'It's absolutely great. **Very funny**.'
The Teaching Booth

'Absolutely loved this story. **5* from us**.'
Amie, age 9, *Toppsta*

'Full of heart and giggles.'
My Book Corner

'A joy to read.'
Leon James, age 11, *Toppsta*

'Love this book . . . full of **fun and mayhem**.'
Poppy, age 6, *Toppsta*

'Funny and quirky.'
Books for Keeps

'Very **entertaining** indeed.'
Alligator's Mouth

'A **JOY** of a book. Loved every page,
gobbled it up in one afternoon.'
Michelle Harrison, author of *A Pinch of Magic*

About the Author

Claire Barker is an author and illustrator living in deepest, darkest Devon. She has lived near the sea for most of her life, several of them on a wild little farm. Claire is the author of animal fantasy series Knitbone Pepper as well as the Picklewitch & Jack series. She sees magic everywhere.

About the Illustrator

Teemu Juhani is a Finnish illustrator, comic artist and graphic designer. Born and raised in a land of snow and northern lights, he grew up holding his pencil and dreaming of superheroes. Currently he's most likely eating some cookies.

The Picklewitch & Jack series

Picklewitch and Jack
Picklewitch & Jack and the Cuckoo Cousin
Picklewitch & Jack and the Sea Wizard's Secret

'Well ...' Jack turned to Picklewitch, bit his lip and said, 'I suppose you don't get to visit a Sea Wizard's cave every day, do you? It might be very educational.'

'I KNEW it!' Picklewitch grinned and shovelled down the last scraps of his pudding. 'You is my best friend and the kipper's knickers too, Jack! We is the best team ever! Midnight picnic here we come!'

Praise for
Picklewitch & Jack

'A **chuckle-filled** story.'
BookTrust

'Couldn't put it down . . . **100% must read**.'
Ame, age 10, *Toppsta*

'Everything about this book is **a joy!**'
Book Lover Jo

'Absolutely **whizz-cracking!**'
The Reader Teacher

'A **great** book to share at bedtime.'
Jemt, age 8, *Toppsta*

'A joy to read aloud.'
Andy Shepherd,
author of *The Boy Who Grew Dragons*

FABER has published children's books since 1929. T. S. Eliot's *Old Possum's Book of Practical Cats* and Ted Hughes' *The Iron Man* were amongst the first. Our catalogue at the time said that 'it is by reading such books that children learn the difference between the shoddy and the genuine'. We still believe in the power of reading to transform children's lives. All our books are chosen with the express intention of growing a love of reading, a thirst for knowledge and to cultivate empathy. We pride ourselves on responsible editing. Last but not least, we believe in kind and inclusive books in which all children feel represented and important.

For my Dad, with love and limpets x

First published in 2021
by Faber & Faber Limited
Bloomsbury House
74–77 Great Russell Street
London, WC1B 3DA
faberchildrens.co.uk

Typeset in Jenson by M Rules
Printed by CPI Group (UK) Ltd, Croydon CR0 4YY
All rights reserved
Text © Claire Barker, 2021
Illustrations © Teemu Juhani, 2021

The right of Claire Barker and Teemu Juhani to be
identified as author and illustrator of this work respectively
has been asserted in accordance with Section 77 of the
Copyright, Designs and Patents Act 1988

A CIP record for this book is available
from the British Library

ISBN 978–0–571–33522–0

FSC
www.fsc.org
MIX
Paper from
responsible sources
FSC® C020471

2 4 6 8 10 9 7 5 3 1

CLAIRE BARKER

Picklewitch & Jack
and the
Sea Wizard's Secret

Illustrated by
Teemu Juhani

faber

1

Hot News

The classroom windows of St Immaculate's School for the Gifted were propped wide open in the summer heat. Golden sunbeams streamed in and draped themselves lazily across the wooden floorboards. Outside, honeybees buzzed, roses bloomed and lawnmowers puttered up and down the perfectly striped lawns.

'FRAZZLIN' FUDGENUTS,' panted Picklewitch. She was sitting with her boots propped up on the desk, fanning herself with a crow feather. 'I'm as hot as a boiled beetroot.'

Jack tried not to stare, but it was true – Picklewitch's face *was* very red and shiny. He wanted to say that she looked much more like a tomato than a beetroot, but he thought better of it. Instead he said, 'Maybe your outfit is the problem.'

Picklewitch looked down at her dungarees and boots. 'What do you mean?'

'Well,' he said, 'you always dress like it's the middle of autumn.'

Picklewitch thought about this for a moment. 'I see,' she said. 'Thank you, Jack.'

Thank you? Was she feeling unwell? Or was she actually listening to his advice for the first time ever?

'What we need here,' declared Picklewitch, groping around in her tatty rucksack for her book of magic, 'is a switchy-witchy change of seasons!

I've got a whizz-cracking spell in my Grim somewhere. Mayhaps a chilly wind,' she said, browsing through the stained pages, 'or some thunder clouds right over the school, like a lovely shady sunhat. Maybe even a thick fog. Then I'll be much more comfortable.'

She sat up, her voice bright. 'I know – I'll call the Stormbeast. He'll freeze the pond and then we can all go skating!'

'No,' sighed Jack, putting his head in his hands. 'That's *not* what I meant at all.'

'Well then, what DO you mean?' she muttered, not bothering to look up, still flicking through the sticky pages of her Grim.

'I mean,' said Jack, feeling exasperated, 'why don't you just take your hat off if you're so hot? Or maybe even your boots?'

'Take my boots off?' Picklewitch turned to look at him in horror. 'WOT a thing to say! I know Boxies have got some strange ideas, Jack, but really! *How dares you?* As IF a witch would EVER take her boots off! Only a stinkfungus would suggest such a thing. Maybe a grubbler or mayhaps a dozypox . . .'

'*All right, all right,* keep your voice down, Picklewitch,' whispered Jack, looking to see if anyone was watching. 'You don't *always* have to use magic, you know. You could just use common sense. You know the rule: *no more spells in school.* We don't want anyone knowing you're a real witch, do we? I'm only trying to help.'

Picklewitch pointed a dirty finger at him. 'Yes,

well, *don't*, because Boxies don't know nothing about the correct temperature for a witch. Just you mind your own beeswax.'

Snorting in disgust, she folded her arms tightly across her chest and a field mouse leapt out of her dungarees pocket. 'What a rude boy. NOBODY tells ME what to do BECUZ . . .' said Picklewitch, beginning her familiar rant, 'I DUZ what I LIKES and I LIKES what I DUZ. So there.' She stuck out her tongue and blew a wet raspberry in his face.

Jack wiped the spit from his eye. Picklewitch, a wild little girl who lived in the walnut tree at the end of his garden, never did what she was told, so why should this time be any different? Whether she was dancing on the roof with the magpies or tangling him up in her magic, she always did exactly what she wanted and it got him in endless trouble.

But even though she stole his cakes, had bird-nest hair and smelled of mushrooms, Jack was very fond of her. Being such a sensible and well-behaved boy, he really couldn't explain why he liked her so much. But then it was also a mystery as to why she had chosen *him* as a best friend – a boy who had only ever spent the long playtimes alone. The truth was, that for all her faults, she was loyal and fun – not to mention as popular as pudding. And he couldn't deny that when Picklewitch was around, exciting things always seemed to happen. After all, how many children could say they were best friends with a little witch?

On cue, Picklewitch opened her grubby fist to reveal a shiny handful of ladybirds. She leaned in close to them and whispered:

'Ladybird ladybird
Rise up and roam,
flutter and putter,
fly away home!'

Jack watched the little bugs unfurl their spotty
wings and whirr like tiny clockwork buttons out
of the window, bound for the garden at Rookery
Heights. His – or rather, Picklewitch's – garden
was a tangled paradise, buzzing, humming and
swishing with life. Birds sang in the trees, frogs
plopped into the pond and shimmering dragonflies
rose up from the overgrown grass. Tucked safely
away behind high brick walls, it was a magical
rambling kingdom with moods that changed like
the wind. The garden was Picklewitch's true home
and sometimes, looking into her leafy-green eyes,
Jack had the uncomfortable feeling that it was

looking straight back at him.

In light of this, perhaps it wasn't surprising that Picklewitch's wildness had wooshed down the corridors of St Immaculate's School for the Gifted since their very first day. Nature had followed Picklewitch to school like an obedient pet. These days nobody raised an eyebrow at the ivy curling through the keyholes and snails munching their way through the books on the shelves.

Jack was counting the caterpillars marching up the curtains when Professor Bright swept into the room. The class, deep in study, sprang immediately to attention.

'Good afternoon, everyone,' said Professor Bright, watering the marigold in his inkwell. 'Goodness, it's hot in here, isn't it? Never mind – I have some *cool* news, ha ha!'

'I hope it's about a new language teacher,'

whispered Aamir Patel, pushing his spectacles up the bridge of his nose and ignoring the joke, 'because I don't think lessons in twenty-four languages is enough.'

Astrid Olsen, Junior Astrophysicist of the year, replied, 'I hope it's new data from the Hubble telescope.'

Fenella gave a wistful sigh: 'Perhaps it's some new Shakespearian texts for the library.'

'*We know what it is!*' chorused the telepathic Wilson twins, fingers pressed on each other's temples in concentration. 'It's a ... it's a ... IT'S A TRIP!'

'Excellent mind work, Wilson twins! Well done!' beamed Professor Bright. 'Your gifts get better and better! You are correct – we are going on a trip to the seaside!'

The whole class beamed, except for Picklewitch

who was far too busy tickling an earwig.

'We are very lucky,' continued Professor Bright, his voice rising over the tide of thrilled whisperings, 'that world-renowned scientist, author *and* ex-pupil of St Immaculate's – Dr Firenza Sharptooth – has extended her yearly invitation to Draconis Hall, her cliff-top home and study centre in Dorset. As I'm sure you all know, Dorset is on the Jurassic Coast, an area famous for remarkable fossil finds.'

Jack almost leapt out of his chair in excitement. Firstly, he was a huge fan of fossils – even having his own collection in his bedroom. Secondly, *of course* he'd heard of the famous Firenza Sharptooth. She had written his favourite book on the subject. She was an adventurer, a scientist and brilliantly clever – she was his hero! This was the best news ever.

'Sir, sir!' he asked, his hand reaching for the sky

and his words tumbling over each other in a rush. 'Will we get the chance to meet her in person? Will she sign my copy of *Fabulous Fossils*? Will we be allowed to dig for fossils of our own and show them to her?'

'Yes, yes, Jack,' chuckled Professor Bright. 'Settle down. We will be looking at how the cliffs on this coastline hold the key to millions of years of history, and there will be plenty of opportunity to discover your own treasures. In fact, there is to be a competition, with a prize for the most remarkable find.'

The whole class sat up at the word 'competition'. Accustomed to being the best in their chosen subject, they *loved* a chance to compete.

'This year's prize is truly remarkable,' continued Professor Bright. 'The winner will receive *a Bonestar* – a top-of-the-range steel fossil hammer.

Not only this, the handle will be signed by Dr Firenza Sharptooth herself.'

Jack had to steady himself. 'Picklewitch,' he said, 'did you hear that?' He was hardly able to contain his delight. '*A Bonestar hammer signed by Dr Firenza Sharptooth*! It's a dream come true. A field trip, a competition and a prize. Aren't you excited?'

Picklewitch yawned and scratched her nose. 'Well, not really, Jack, 'cos you see I've already been in lots of fields.'

'No, a *field trip*,' laughed Jack. 'It's like a study holiday.' There was a long silence as he realised she didn't know what he was talking about. 'Picklewitch, you *have* been on holiday before, haven't you?'

'*Yes.*' Picklewitch gave an awkward snort and smirk. 'A-course I has. What a silly thing to ask.'

'Where?'

'Places.'

'What places?'

'Lossa places. Anyway,' she sighed, slipping her boots off the desk top, 'I don't see the point. The birds go away every year and you know what? They only end up coming back again, like they are all giddy widdershins and can't make up their mind. As it happens, *I* is far too busy to go a-gallivanting off on some *holiday*. Some of us have got work to do.'

'Oh come on, Picklewitch! Fossils are wonders of Nature! The air is much cooler by the seaside too.' he added, looking at her red face.

'No. It's out of the question,' she said. 'I am far too busy with important garden business.' She began to reel off a long list of excuses on her grubby fingertips, one by one. 'For example, only the other day there was all sorts of fudgenuttery among the robins. Then there's Basher Crunch. He'll be out of badger jail any day now. Plus, what if I leave my tree and the leaves go all droopy and sad? Also, the most important of these twelve Very Important Facts is that my garden is the best place in the world, so why would I want to leave it? No, it makes no sense at all. No. My brain would have to be made of jelly. No.'

Jack pleaded. 'But it'll be brilliant! Why not try something new? I'm sure the garden can look after itself for a few days.'

Picklewitch puffed herself up like a pigeon. 'Oh, it *can*, can it? Well, that just shows what *you* know.' She picked up her rucksack, slung it onto her back in a huff and climbed up onto the windowsill. 'Witches have got rezpondabilities. If you want to go an' grubble in the dirt, far away from bestest friends and sparrows and Ladymum's cakes, you're more of a fopdoodle than I thought.'

'Hey! Where are you going?' cried Jack. 'It's not even home time yet!'

Picklewitch jumped straight out of the classroom window and stomped off across the school fields without so much as a backwards glance, squirrels scampering at her boot heels.

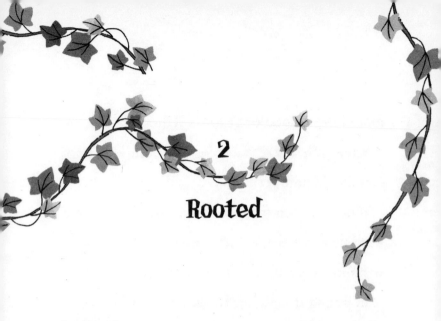

2

Rooted

The evening before the field trip, Jack spent a long time packing and repacking his suitcase, being very concerned that he might leave something important behind. He was on his ninth repack when Picklewitch leapt in through his attic bedroom window, making him jump.

'PICKLEWITCH!' he cried, clasping at his heart. 'Why can't you just come through the front door like a normal person?'

'Stairs and doors and suchlike fandangling

trumpery is for Boxie house-dwellers like you, not witches,' she said. '*Witches* only use proper official trees and drainpipes.'

Knowing this was an argument he couldn't possibly win, Jack turned his attention back to his suitcase.

'Right,' he said, pressing down the items in the bulging case, 'I think I've whittled it down to the bare essentials. I've included socks, spare socks and emergency socks, twelve t-shirts, nine pairs of trousers, five pairs of shorts, six jumpers, four pairs of pyjamas, an umbrella, wellingtons, sandals, trainers, flip flops, boots, raincoat, sunhat, sun cream, fiction books, non-fiction books and a French dictionary.' Suddenly anxious, he looked up at Picklewitch, who was sitting on the windowsill, swinging her stripy legs back and forth. 'Do you think I've packed enough? We'll be gone for two whole days.'

'I don't think you should go at all,' said Picklewitch, picking at her teeth with the point of a quill. 'I'm afraid I have some very bad news, Jack. The sparrows tell me there are froshus beasts in Dorset. Nasty, big, murdery ones that like the taste of boys.' She pointed at his overflowing case. 'Especially finicky fusspots, which, unfortunately for you, is their favourite flavour.'

'I know what you are up to, Picklewitch, and it won't work,' said Jack, shutting the lid of his case with some difficulty. 'I wouldn't miss this trip for anything, ferocious beasts or not.' He pointed to the fossils lined up in a neat row on his bedroom shelf. 'I've been collecting those since I was little. It's time for me to discover a remarkable fossil of my own and YOU are not going to stop me.'

Picklewitch let out a feeble cough and fluttered

her eyelashes. 'But Jack, I think you should know that I've got a deadly poorliness and *coff* I probably won't make it past Friday teatime. And I've also got an ache in my knee from feeling sad, not to mention a draught in my eye.'

Jack zipped up the case. 'You are fit as a fiddle, Picklewitch. I'm going to the seaside and that's that.'

Scowling, Picklewitch slithered off the windowsill and crossed over to Jack's fossil collection. She picked one up and gave it a lick. 'So, this a fizzle, is it?'

Jack rushed over, prising it from her hand. 'Be careful! It's a *fossil*, not a fizzle, and it's millions of years old. It's called an ammonite. Don't you think it's beautiful?'

'Looks just like a rock to me,' said Picklewitch, inspecting it. 'Don't see what's so special about it. I've got lots of funny pebbles in my garden. I've got one that looks like an egg, one that looks like a shoe, and one shaped just like a fox's wotsit. I'll give it to you if you don't go.'

'No thank you,' said Jack, placing the ammonite back on the shelf.

Picklewitch slumped to the floor, crossing her legs and arms. She uncrossed them and then crossed them again. She huffed and puffed, shuffled on her bottom and drummed her fingers on the floorboards. 'So . . . you're just going to leave me and the garden and Ladymum all alone then, are you? What if danger occurs?'

'You're the only danger likely to occur around here, Picklewitch.'

'But . . . oh . . . but . . . but *I duzzant want you*

to go!' wailed Picklewitch, tugging her hat down around her ears. 'Who will I talk to? Who will I play with? You can't go.'

'Tough, because I AM going.'

Picklewitch stood up and stamped her foot on the floorboards, steam escaping from her earholes. 'FUDGENUTS AND SPADGER'S PANTS!' She was about to launch into a full-scale tantrum when her magpie eye suddenly caught sight of a pile of shining coins on Jack's bedside.

'Oh thanks,' said Jack, following her gaze. 'I nearly forgot.' He scooped the money into his trouser pocket. 'Money for ice creams.'

'*I-screams?*' Picklewitch licked her lips and wiggled her eyebrows. 'Did you say *I-screams?* Like the ones from the jingly van? Cold as snow? Pink and brown and yellow and white? With red sauce and chocolate sticks and rainbow sprinkles?'

'Yes.'

'But Picklewitch loves I-screams.'

'I thought you only liked cake,' Jack said.

Picklewitch pouted. 'You never mentioned *I-screams.*'

'The seaside is famous for them, but of course you would know that,' said Jack, 'having been on *so many holidays.*'

Picklewitch's mood switched in the blink of an eye. 'Jack, you will be glad to know I have changed my mind. I SHALL be coming to the seaside after all, so that I can keep a close eye on you and your fizzling fields. You can't possibly win that prize without my help. I'll say it *once* and then I'll say it *again*: you are such a lucky boy to have me as a friend.'

She climbed back up onto the windowsill and shouted out into the trees. 'Birds – pack my bag!'

Then she leapt out of the open window into the black night. 'WOO HOO!' she squealed, landing with a thump in a bush. 'Picklewitch is going on holiday!'

3

Buckle Up Buttercup

Jack looked nervously at his watch. A fan of punctuality and following the rules, he thought the letter had been very clear. The minibus was picking them up outside his garden gate at 8:45 am precisely. It would be here in only four minutes and seventeen seconds, and there was *still* no sign of Picklewitch. He took out his journal and checked the list for the twentieth time. Kiss mum goodbye? *Check.* Suitcase packed? *Check.* Waterproof, rucksack, wellies? *Check.* He looked left, right, up and behind. *Where WAS she?*

Finally, the garden door creaked open and Picklewitch struggled through the gap, her hat wonky and ivy clinging desperately to her ankles.

'There you are!' cried Jack in relief. 'I was worried you weren't coming.'

'Course I am,' she muttered, turning to bolt the door behind her. 'But the garden's not taken the news well. I've had bindweed tangling around me and weepy sparrows to deal with. The Stormbeast's been drizzling and wailing all night, and my tree has definitely gone droopy. I said *I'll only be gone two days* and left strict instructions – eggs must be turned in the nests, the bird bath is to be filled and in no circumstances is anyone to fight the owls, no matter how much they deserve it. And here, you forgot this . . .' Picklewitch handed him his lunchbox in a bag.

Jack was confused, sure he'd already packed

it. Before he could think any more about it Picklewitch said, 'Oh look!' pointing her finger up the street. 'It's the minibus. Chop-chop, Jack! We haven't got all day.'

The school minibus pulled up next to the kerb, brimming with smiling faces. Angus Pilkington-Storm waved his school scarf like they were on their way to a rugby match and sobby Fenella held up her toy owl. The minibus door rolled back with a clunk to reveal Professor Bright at the wheel. He waved at them.

'Hop in you two,' he said. 'It's a long journey to the seaside.'

Jack hauled his heavy suitcase into the boot and then took a seat. Picklewitch climbed in too, uncertain what to do next.

Jack patted the seat next to him. 'Sit here, Picklewitch, next to me.' He realised that she had

never travelled inside a bus before, much
preferring to ride on the roof, the wind in
her hair. 'Why don't you sit next to this
open window, close to the fresh air?'

Picklewitch sat down reluctantly
and, after a bit of a tussle, he managed
to wrestle her into her seatbelt.
Soon she was clicking it in and out,
delighted by the sound. In no time
they were on the road, zooming
towards the seaside.

'So, Picklewitch,' he said in a breezy manner, 'what's in your packed lunch?'

Picklewitch looked very alarmed indeed. '*My* packed lunch?'

Victoria sniggered and looked sideways at the others. Victoria, master baker, was the only pupil at St Immaculate's who disliked Picklewitch. 'Picklewitch is *such* a weirdo,' she giggled. 'Doesn't even know you're supposed to bring a packed lunch on a school trip!'

Picklewitch smiled at Victoria in a very unsmiley way. 'Better buckle up nice and tight, Bossy Baker. Don't want you to come to no *harm*.'

Immediately suspicious, Victoria looked down at her seatbelt. A large yellow python was slinking around her middle, squeezing tight. 'EEEEEE!' she shrieked, frantically pressing herself into the back of the seat. 'Help, HELP! A SNAKE!'

Professor Bright glanced over his shoulder. 'What on earth is the matter, girl?' he barked.

Victoria looked down again. 'But ... but ... the snake! It was there just a minute ago. Didn't anyone else see it?' Everyone shook their heads.

Victoria gritted her teeth and jabbed a finger in Picklewitch's direction. 'WITCH!' she roared. 'I'll get you for this! She must have put one of her spells on me! I told you, but no one will listen! She shouldn't even be allowed on this trip. I shall be letting my parents know.'

'Don't talk such nonsense, child,' tutted Professor Bright, his eyes fixed on the road. 'Picklewitch has as much right to be here as anyone. And I am getting rather tired of having to explain to you that there are no such things as real witches. It simply isn't logical, nor is the idea that a snake might suddenly appear on a minibus.

Perhaps you are unwell. Perhaps YOU are the one that should have stayed at home.'

'That told her,' said Jack, smiling at Picklewitch. 'Don't worry about your packed lunch – you can have some of my mine.' He reached down for his lunchbox to show her all the delicious things he had brought, but to his surprise it was empty.

'Where's it gone?' He opened the lid and looked inside at the empty cake wrappers. 'Where are my little cheese sandwiches? The fruit? All the cupcakes?' Picklewitch looked away and pressed her nose firmly against the window.

Jack tapped her on the shoulder. 'Picklewitch, *where* is my lunch?'

'Well, goodness. How rude. I don't knows to what you is referring.' She let out a little burp. 'Pudding me.'

Not again. Picklewitch was always taking Jack's

food when he was distracted. 'Give me my lunch back,' he hissed in her ear. 'And don't get clever with me. I don't want any of your worm sandwiches or frogspawn jelly. I want my own proper food.'

'OH LOOK!' cried Picklewitch, pointing out of the window at a traffic sign. 'I spy a D for dragon!'

Jack rolled his eyes. 'You're just trying to distract me. There's no such things as dragons.'

'Hey, everyone!' said Aamir. 'That's a great idea of Picklewitch's! Let's play I Spy to pass the time!'

Everyone cheered. As this was St Immaculate's School for the Gifted, the game went on for ages because all the clues were in Latin or in a numbered code.

Meanwhile, Picklewitch, who hadn't the faintest idea what I Spy was, took the opportunity to scoff the contents of everyone else's lunchboxes, snaffling the lot while no one was looking. By the time they arrived in Dorset she was as plump as a pumpkin, had had a super snooze, a smashing snore and decided she should go on holiday more often.

When the minibus eventually pulled into the driveway of Draconis Hall, everyone was tired and very hungry. Night was falling and the severe grey stone Victorian building loomed over them like an ominous shadow. As Jack hauled his big suitcase out of the minibus, he noticed the gargoyles looking down on them from the gutters, their mouths open wide, as if caught mid-roar. Draconis Hall was not quite as welcoming as he had imagined.

4

Bedward to the Greenwood

After dinner everyone went to the dormitories to unpack. There was much squabbling over who should get the top bunks. Jack managed to nab a bed next to the window, so that Picklewitch would have the best view of the garden. He lay down on the bottom bunk while Picklewitch bounced up and down on the mattress above him, the bedsprings squeaking. 'This nest is most peculiar, even for a Boxie. I don't like it,' she said, appearing over the edge and hanging upside down like a bat.

'It's called a bunk bed,' whispered Jack. 'Don't be so ungrateful . . . and keep your voice down. You're not even supposed to be in the boys' dorm.'

'Bonkers bed more like. Very odd,' Picklewitch said, swinging side to side. 'It's not the only weird thing either. Everything here is strange and wrong. I feels it in my bones. I miss my tree and the birds and the wind. I want to go home.'

Jack smiled. 'But we've only just arrived, Picklewitch. Don't worry – you're just a bit homesick, that's all. This is what happens on holiday; you have to get used to sleeping in different places, with different smells and sounds. Soon it will feel perfectly normal. Have you unpacked yet?'

Picklewitch reached down for her rucksack and tipped it upside down like a bin. A jumble of rubbish fell out with a clatter; empty yoghurt pots and cake wrappers, her Grim, some walnuts and her cracked binoculars. 'As you can see,' she said, 'the birds have thought of everything.'

Loud footsteps rang out over the wooden floorboards as Victoria appeared in the doorway. 'Ah, Picklewitch. There you are.'

'Here we go,' sighed Jack.

'You do know you're not allowed to sleep in here with Jack, don't you?' said Victoria, marching towards them. 'You have to sleep with the girls at the end of the corridor. This is a dormitory for boys. YOU ...' she looked Picklewitch up and down with some distaste, 'may be many things, but you are *not* a boy.'

Picklewitch somersaulted down onto the floor, her boots landing on the wooden boards with a thud. '*YOU* should be more careful,' she whispered in menacing tones, standing nose to nose with

Victoria. *'Because you don't know WHAT I iz.'*

Victoria's mouth flapped like a flip-top bin. She looked like she was about to say something, but then thought better of it. Instead she span on her shiny heel and marched back out of the dormitory.

'Stupid Bossy Baker. No one tells me what to do. I'll sleep where I like,' muttered Picklewitch, shoving everything back in her rucksack. 'Which is why I'm not sleeping in this horrible old house like some bloomin' Boxie, bonkers bed or not.' She took her own pulse and felt her forehead. Her eyes widened in dismay. 'Oh no, I knew it! I've gone and caught a bad case of homesickness.'

'But …' protested Jack weakly, 'we all have to sleep inside. It's the rules.'

A small flock of yellow-eyed seagulls had lined up on the windowsill, slapping their feet and pecking at the glass, *rat-a-tat-tat*. Picklewitch

peered over their bobbing heads down into the twilight of the gardens. 'All right, I'm coming. Time to roost.' She opened the sash window and grabbed a vine of ivy. 'Bedward to the greenwood!' she cried, swooping out into the night.

Once upon a time this would have caused Jack to worry, but not now. *Picklewitch is as wild as a blackbird,* he thought as he pulled on his NASA pyjamas and brushed his teeth (ninety-four brushes down, ninety-four brushes up). *I'll bet the garden here is large and old with plenty of trees. She'll simply find a comfy mossy branch to sleep on and a baby bat to cuddle up to. She'll be bossing the birds about by breakfast.*

Jack put his toothbrush away and zipped up his washbag. He climbed into the bottom bunk and yawned, just as Professor Bright popped his head around the door.

'Everybody found a bunk and unpacked?' he asked, looking at the rows of heads. 'Excellent. Exciting day tomorrow! Fossils and fun galore. You'll need a good night's sleep. Goodnight, boys. Lights out!' Then, with the flick of a switch, the room was suddenly dark.

'Goodnight, sir!' the boys chorused. As the sound of footsteps disappeared down the corridor, a dozen torches clicked on as everyone pulled out their secret bedtime reading.

Jack took out a beloved copy of *Fabulous Fossils* by Dr Firenza Sharptooth from under his pillow. He clicked on his own torch and settled back into his pillow. But just as he was getting stuck into the well-thumbed chapter on Ichthyosaurs, his thoughts momentarily strayed back to Picklewitch. He hoped she was all right out there in a strange new garden. He hoped she would enjoy finding fossils with him tomorrow. He hoped she wouldn't feel lonely … but mostly? Mostly he hoped the fresh sea air would wear her out.

5

Porridge and Prizes

Next morning Picklewitch appeared in the dining room, hobbling and clutching her bottom.

'Morning, Picklewitch,' said Jack. 'How did you sleep?'

Picklewitch muttered and tutted.

'Oh dear,' said Jack, pushing out a chair. 'Do you want to sit down?'

Picklewitch gave the chair a rueful glance and shook her head.

'What's wrong?' asked Jack.

'What is *wrong*,' whispered Picklewitch, looking from side to side to check that no one was listening, 'is that I had a tree accident last night.'

'A tree accident?' asked Jack. 'What's that?'

'Seagulls bet me I couldn't sleep in a Monkey Puzzle tree.'

Jack thought carefully. 'But aren't they the really, really spiky ones? The ones with thorns all up the trunk and along the branches?'

Picklewitch busily stuffed her pockets with toast and buns from the breakfast buffet. She took a ladleful of porridge and dolloped it into her front pocket. 'Like sleeping in a sack of hedgehogs. Here's a piece of advice for free, Jack: never trust a seagull. Fudgenuts and mudlarks; proper naughty birds they are. Think they're funny, laughing themselves silly.'

'Oops,' said Jack, desperately trying to hold in a

laugh as he noticed a gang of seagulls lining up along the windowsills, slapping their feet and cackling.

Picklewitch slurped marmalade out of the little pots. 'You better not be laughing too, or else.'

Jack was saved from having to reply when Professor Bright stood up at the front of the dining hall.

'Good morning, children,' he said, straightening his gowns and smoothing his hair down. 'Today is a very exciting day! A day of exploration and adventure. But before we begin, I have the *very great pleasure* of introducing you to our host and the owner of this magnificent house.' Professor Bright gestured to a door on his left labelled 'LIBRARY'. 'I give you fossil expert and best-selling author, the one and only – Dr FIRENZA SHARPTOOTH!' With this, the door swung open and everyone broke into excited applause.

A tall woman wearing a black velvet cloak and an eye patch stepped out and glided over to join the professor at the top table. What an entrance! Jack clapped until his hands tingled, overcome with the thrill of actually seeing his hero in the flesh. She looked even better than he had imagined – like a beautiful and brilliant science-pirate.

'Good morning, children,' she said, taking in the smiling faces around the room. 'Thank you, dearest Professor Bright. I am delighted to welcome St Immaculate's School for the Gifted to Draconis Hall once more. An ex-pupil myself, I am aware that I am in a room of exceptional young minds. Who knows? Maybe someone here will make a brand new discovery!' Jack clutched his copy of *Fabulous Fossils* so tightly that his hand tingles turned into full-blown pins and needles.

Dr Sharptooth pointed to a display cabinet above her head, packed with fossils. 'This house,' she said, 'has been in the Sharptooth family for over a hundred years. As I'm sure you are aware, I come from a long line of explorers with a passion for discovery; geologists and palaeontologists . . .'

'Paleytollyjists?' whispered Picklewitch. 'Is it people wot do like pale things? Like the moon? 'Cos Picklewitch likes both the moon *and* the bear wot does live on it.'

'Shut up. No, of course not,' hissed Jack. 'Palaeontologist. It means dinosaur expert. Shh!'

'This area is a treasure trove of fossils,' continued Dr Sharptooth. 'A World Heritage site, its cliffs are full of clues to our planet's past; layers upon layers of history. Many of the earliest discoveries of dinosaur and other prehistoric remains have been unearthed here. Indeed, this is the very place where Mary Anning, one of the greatest fossilists of all time, made her most important discoveries. Mary proves to us that anyone can be a fossil hunter – indeed, she helped uncover an Ichthyosaur when she was only twelve.' The room filled with mutters and Dr Sharptooth raised her hand for silence. 'However, remember this: if you find anything *unusual*, anything of *interest*, you must bring it to me straight away. Do you understand? On these beaches, a clever child can stumble across wonders; incredible, fantastic creatures that have been hidden for millions of years. You will need an expert eye to inspect your finds.'

A buzz of excited whispers raced around the room again. 'So, to the challenge,' smiled Dr Sharptooth. 'This year's prize is a *Bonestar hammer* – the very best fossil-hunting instrument money can buy. It is the ultimate addition to any serious collector's tool kit.' A mahogany box stood next to her on the table. She leaned over, clicked its clasps and pulled out a shiny steel hammer. 'A remarkable prize for a remarkable discovery.'

Jack's imagination was out of the starting gate like a whippet. In his mind's eye he could see it all: him proudly accepting the hammer, Dr Firenza Sharptooth tearful with emotion, the articles in scientific journals, the brass nameplate in the British Natural History Museum ...

'Jackosaurus'
Dinosaur skeleton
Dorset. England.

This lovely daydream was rudely interrupted when Picklewitch raised her hand.

'Excuse me.'

Oh no. Jack felt his whole body go rigid with fear.

'Yes, may I help you?' Dr Firenza Sharptooth peered at the girl standing at the back, who appeared to be rubbing her bottom while porridge trickled out of her trouser leg.

'I got questions. Number one: where are the I-screams?'

Dr Sharptooth looked very confused. 'I beg your pardon?'

'You heard what I said. Number two: I'll be needing you to give me that Bonestirrer right now.' She put her arm around Jack, who shrank away from her embrace like a salted slug. 'It's not for me. It's for my best friend here.'

'Ah, I see, a joke!' Dr Sharptooth laughed. 'I'm afraid I can't just GIVE you the prize. You would have to win it first. That's the point, you see? It's a competition. Anything else would be cheating.'

'Yes, well,' said Picklewitch, most matter-of-factly, 'I knows *that*. That's the point.'

'*Picklewitch, please stop*,' begged Jack, sliding under the table in shame.

'Stop? But why?' asked Picklewitch, bending down to look at him. 'You *know* how important cheating is to a witch. You like to win and I like to cheat – we're the perfect team!'

'Children, children!' Professor Bright clapped his hands loudly, keen to change the subject. 'I'm sure you are *all* hoping to win the prize. But first, much work must be done. Please gather your kit and we shall meet at the front of the house, ready to walk down to the beach and begin our seaside adventure and fabulous fossil hunt!'

6

Lonestar

It was a gorgeous day, bright and blue. The sea sparkled in the distance and a heat shimmer was already rising from the ground. The beach was only a short walk from the house and the children, dressed in fluorescent yellow bibs that made them look like ducklings, marched off down the cliff path, wellington boots slapping at the backs of their bare legs, *flip-flap-flop*. Professor Bright led the group, holding up a banner with the school's lion crest on it, like a giant sandcastle flag. They walked in a line carrying all the necessary equipment: tape measures, books, brushes, hammers, buckets and clipboards. Jack couldn't resist bringing all the essential extras, just in case, including Plaster of Paris, a hard hat, goggles, a ruler, his journal and a compass. Struggling somewhat under the weight, he looked around for Picklewitch to assist him. But as soon as the words *please form an orderly queue* were mentioned, she had evaporated like the morning mist.

Typical of Picklewitch to disappear just as the proper work starts, thought Jack, climbing carefully down the steps onto the beach. *So much for 'the perfect team'. Never mind, she'd only distract me from my serious scientific work anyway. Magic is never required when undergoing a thorough investigation of the facts.*

Picklewitch had no time for

science, something that caused Jack endless frustration. He had explained why she was wrong on many occasions, but Picklewitch had her own extremely strong opinions on the matter. Privately though, Jack had to admit it was difficult to argue with someone who could turn herself into a pine cone.

Professor Bright clapped his hands. 'Right, children. Here is a list of fossils you may find,' he said, passing around worksheets on clipboards. 'Ammonites, Brachiopods and Coprolites, etc. We are expecting great things! Small safety announcement first – do keep an eye on the tide and watch out for rock falls. They are very common in this area so please stay away from the cliffs. Feel free to explore, but *always* keep this flag in sight so you don't get lost.' He stuck the long flagpole into the sand. 'We have 250 million years of history at our feet so let's waste no more time – the great fossil hunt is on!' With the shrill blow of a whistle, the children scattered along the beach like shells.

Jack was about to begin when his attention was drawn to a pair of seagulls standing on a bin, squabbling and squawking over a discarded ice-cream cone. One of them turned and stared straight at him, winked a suspiciously green eye and flapped off.

Was that her? Was she stealing ice creams? Jack gave himself a shake and whispered, 'Focus, Jack. Stop thinking about what Picklewitch is up to and concentrate on why you're here. That hammer won't win itself. Get down to work.'

He scanned the length of the beach. First of all he needed to assess the competition. The Wilson twins were already chipping away, taking turns to bash at a large chunk of rock, *donk-DONK donk-DONK*. Astrid and Angus were busy cordoning off a section of the beach with stripy tape that said 'DO NOT ENTER: SCIENTIFIC INVESTIGATION IN PROGRESS'. Fenella and Aamir were measuring rocks and scribbling down notes. Everybody else already seemed to be in partners. Everybody, that is, except for Victoria, who sat beneath a parasol, eating a cake and reading a baking magazine. He'd rather eat worms than partner up with her. Jack set off down the beach alone, hoping to find a peaceful spot further away to conduct his important research.

Eventually, when the flag was nothing but a small dot in the distance, Jack stopped. He carefully took his equipment and reference books out of his rucksack, methodically laid them out in alphabetical order and settled down to a morning of quiet, solitary work.

An uneventful couple of hours passed in this way when his ears caught the sound of something on the breeze.

SHE sells SEA shells on the SEAshore,
SEAshore shells sells SHE

Jack stood up and strained to listen. What was that?

And the SEA shells SHE sells on the seashore,
Are SEAshore shells I'm SURE.

There it was again! Was it singing? Jack took out his binoculars and peered into the distance.

Far away he could see splashing, seagulls circling
and a tell-tale black pointy hat. Despite himself,
his heart lifted and he set off along the beach
towards it.

7

Water Baby

As Jack got closer he could see Picklewitch sitting in a shallow rock pool, splashing wildly and singing her head off.

Jack couldn't help but stare. 'What *are* you wearing?'

Picklewitch stopped splashing and looked down at herself. Black and white striped, the less-than-flattering knitted swimming costume sagged in all the wrong places. He noticed she was still wearing her boots too. 'You said I should dress for the weather, so I did.'

'Where did you get it from?' asked Jack, immediately suspicious.

'From the history shop.'

'History shop?' Jack thought for a minute about what she could mean ... then it dawned on him. *Oh no.* 'Do you mean the museum?'

With a little smirk, Picklewitch raised her own binoculars to her eyes and peered at him. 'Mayhaps. Mayhaps not.'

'But things are supposed to stay IN the museum. That is the whole point. Picklewitch, I hope you didn't steal it because, as I have told you *many* times, stealing is very wrong.'

'Couldn't possibly say,' breezed Picklewitch. 'Anyway, I learned lots of interesting facts in there. For a start, there be other witches on this beach.'

Jack scoffed at the idea. 'Don't be silly.'

'Tis true. While you was scraping and dusting,

the lady in the history shop told me all about a witch called Mary. She said she found magical things on the beach and sold 'em to silly Boxies. Struck by britey lightning when she was a baby. She's famous too, like what proper witches should be.'

Jack tutted. 'You mean Mary Anning, the one Dr Sharptooth was talking about at breakfast. No, no, Picklewitch, she wasn't a witch, she was an amazing fossilist. The curiosities were actually ammonites and even dinosaur remains!' Jack went to reach into his bag for his book. 'I could teach you all about her if you'd like.'

Picklewitch plucked a pair of pearly periwinkles out of the rock pool and stuck them to her earlobes. 'No thank you. I don't need some silly Boxie boy to explain what a witch *is* and what a witch is *not*, thank you very much.'

Jack felt annoyed. 'Now listen here, Picklewitch, I simply must correct you on this. Mary Anning is a respected scientist. This sort of attitude is very unhelpful. She absolutely, definitely, *certainly* wasn't a witch.'

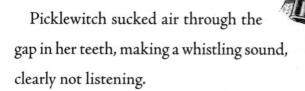

Picklewitch sucked air through the gap in her teeth, making a whistling sound, clearly not listening.

'Anyway,' he continued, 'I have made some excellent progress in my research today, Picklewitch, which I hope you might be interested in. I have been very busy.'

'Yes, well, you're not the only one who's been busy, as you can see.' She waved in the direction of a big nest she had made out of driftwood, shells and bottle tops. Jack noticed that she had written KATS R FUDGENUTS in the sand with a stick.

Jack pressed on. 'I have recorded this data in my journal for when I am director of the British Natural History Museum. You know, I think that if you bothered to take an interest in fossils you would learn a lot and perhaps enjoy this holiday more.'

'Yeah?' said Picklewitch doubtfully, sticking a starfish to the front of her costume. 'Like wot?'

'Like these cliffs, for a start!' He pointed at the crumbling cliffs behind them. 'They record 250 million years of history. All the different layers tell us about animals and plants, many long dead and extinct.'

Picklewitch giggled. 'Well they would stink, wouldn't they, if they been dead awhile?' She thought for a moment. 'Badger Basher Crunch isn't dead, but he proper stinks like a manky old haddock.'

Jack squeezed his eyes shut and concentrated on reciting the introduction to *Fabulous Fossils*: '*These cliffs are the birthplace of a whole new science. The formations in the cliff are full of clues to the past, like a fascinating layer cake.*'

'Cake?' Picklewitch snorted with laughter. 'They don't look much like cake to me. If they were, then all the animals and birds and me wouldn't have to eat out of the bins, would we? Honestly, Jack, you do say the silliest things sometimes. And while we're on that very subject, I have noticed a definite lack of cake since I've arrived. I am missing Ladymum's cakes. I have become *quite thin*.' She burped and a tiny fish hopped out of her mouth.

Jack felt very fed up. It had been a mistake asking Picklewitch to come on holiday with him. She was as stubborn and infuriating as a wart and was spoiling the whole thing with her stupid ideas. But the real reason for his irritation was something else. No matter what he'd told Picklewitch, he hadn't made a single interesting fossil discovery that day. At this rate there was no way he was ever going to impress Dr Firenza Sharptooth, never mind win the Bonestar hammer.

Jack was dwelling on his unhappy situation when Picklewitch suddenly sat bolt upright in her rock pool, her starfish falling off with a splash. She lifted her nose to sniff and snort at the wind. 'Well, well. Blow me down – a whiff of magic already! And it's a rare one too.' She raised her binoculars again and focused them on a lone figure shambling along the shoreline.

Sensing they had been spotted, the figure spun around, took out a telescope and squinted back.

'Would you believe it?' cried Picklewitch. 'Only the first day and I've caught a genuine Sea Wizard! Come on!' She grabbed her rucksack and began to skip across the rocks, her costume dripping and sagging, periwinkles and limpets clinging to her boots.

'A Sea Wizard?' *Oh no. Oh dear.* 'Picklewitch, stop!' cried Jack, abandoning his equipment and racing after her. 'Wait for me!'

8

Manners Matter

The salty stranger quickly scuttled in the opposite direction, but this didn't deter Picklewitch, who broke into a jaunty trot. 'Coo-ee! Sea Wizard!' she called, holding tightly to her hat with one hand and waving cheerfully with the other. She raced down to the low tide line, her shouts getting louder and louder as she got closer to her target:

Sky and land
Monkey gizzard

Foam and sand
YOU'RE a Wizard
I spied you now
You know the code
invite me to
your nice abode
Won't get far
Seashell clatter
Stop right there
'Coz manners matter!'

At this last line, the stranger stopped in their tracks, shoulders slumped in defeat.

Jack tried to keep up with Picklewitch, bracing himself for what they might find. He really didn't have time to get mixed up with Picklewitch's kind right now. They only spelled trouble in his experience. He hoped this boy wasn't going to be as bad as Picklewitch's cousin.

But as they got closer, Jack was surprised to discover that this person wasn't a boy, or even a child. On her head she wore a yellow sou'wester, only it was rather more pointed than usual, and it was crammed over a foamy-frazzle of pearly white hair with fronds of seaweed plaited into it. Brown and as wrinkled as a nut, the Sea Wizard looked like a tiny, grumpy grandma.

In spite of the heat, the old lady was bundled up in rainbow-striped woollies with fishermen's oilskins over the top, studded with barnacles. On her feet were wellington boots overflowing with seawater, while little fish hopped in and out. Finally, swinging around her neck was the most magnificent ammonite fossil Jack had ever seen.

Picklewitch and the Sea Wizard circled each other like cats until, eventually, the older one

broke the silence. 'Well, well,' said the old lady, her eyes as shiny and blue as the sea behind her. 'Seagulls warned me there was trespassers about.'

'Trespassers? Goodness me,' tutted Picklewitch, her leafy-green eyes flashing. 'That's not terribly polite, is it? I think you knows that that's not how you are supposed to behave when a witch arrives for a lovely surprise visit. What about the Code?'

The Sea Wizard let out a long, begrudging sigh. '*Fine,*' she muttered. She gripped her hat and bowed deeply. 'Greetings, Tree Witch, I hope you is well,' she said, forcing a smile through gritted teeth. 'My name is Scowling Margaret. What a nice surprise to see you here on my beach. I should be most honoured if you would please-thankyou come to tea at my most splendiferous sea cave. We can scoff a slice of cake and chit and chat about this and that.'

Picklewitch bowed deeply in return and a winkle rolled out of her costume onto the sand. 'Why *thank you*, Scowling Margaret, and might I say what an honour it is to meet you,' she replied. 'How generous and kind you are! My name is Picklewitch and this 'ere is Jack.' She kicked him in the ankle. 'Say hello to the nice Sea Wizard, Jack.'

Scowling Margaret looked Jack up and down in surprise, as if noticing him for the first time. 'Is it a pet?'

'Of course I'm not a pet!' blurted Jack, shocked by the suggestion.

The Sea Wizard gave him a curious sniff. 'Hmm. His hair is very *clean* for a pet,' muttered Scowling Margaret, as if she hadn't heard him.

'I AM NOT A PET!' repeated Jack. 'Picklewitch, tell her.'

Picklewitch smirked and wagged her finger.

'Now, now, you naughty Sea Wizard, there's no need for your cheek.' She patted Jack on the head. 'Anyway, he can't help being so peculiar. Poor thing has spent all his life in a house.'

'How curious and sad,' said Scowling Margaret. 'I do hope he's not a biter.' She pulled an hourglass out of her pocket and gave it a shake. 'The tide is turning. I have to go. Come back at midnight – don't be late.'

Picklewitch hitched up her swimming costume and grinned widely. 'Most kind, I'm sure. I must say I am looking forward to a bit of that whizz-cracking cake of yours. I am very happy to have met you, Scowling Margaret.'

'I am also very happy,' muttered the Sea Wizard, without the slightest trace of enthusiasm. She spat a bit of seaweed she'd been chewing onto the sand. 'I do so love strangers.' With these parting words she stomped away, galoshes sloshing, until she was nothing but a dot, a flock of seagulls in her wake.

'Well, Jack, at last this rotten holiday is starting to look up,' declared Picklewitch, rubbing her hands together. 'What a result! We've got an invitation to tea, and with a Sea Wizard too!'

'*We?* Oh no, Picklewitch,' protested Jack as they walked back along the beach towards the school flag. 'Absolutely not. I don't have time for this sort of thing. I'm here to discover fossils, not make polite chit-chat with some strange old lady. And midnight? I'm not allowed out whenever I feel like it, you know.' Jack shook his head. 'No, no. It would be far too risky.'

Picklewitch stopped and turned to him in dismay. 'But Jack! You *have* to come or Scowling Margaret will be sad! Didn't you see how much she liked you?'

'Not really,' said Jack, an eyebrow raised. 'She asked if I was your *pet*.'

'Oh really. Pish and posh. You's such a frazzlin' fusspot,' complained Picklewitch, kicking at the seaweed. 'All wizards is a bit moody, 'tis natural. They like to be left alone.'

'So why *aren't* we leaving her alone?' asked Jack.

Picklewitch rolled her eyes. 'I'd have thought that was obvious, even to a Boxie like you. Do I have to spell it out? F R E E C A Y K E.'

Jack sighed and looked anxiously at his watch. He could see the school party further up the beach and gathered up all of his equipment in a hurry.

'Oh go on, Jack, *pleeeze*,' nagged Picklewitch. 'She was wearing a fizzle and everything. I know you saw it,' she wheedled, whispering in his ear. 'I bet you'd like to know where she got it, wouldn't you?' She gave a big wink. 'You might see something else *very special* too if you're lucky.'

Jack looked away, but Picklewitch pressed on with the determination of a mosquito. 'But mostly it's important you come because then I can have your slice of cake too.'

'No, out of the question. Count me out.'

Picklewitch put her hands on her hips and stamped her foot. 'Poppycock and cheese-weasels, if you aren't as selfish as a snail! You made me come on this blooming holiday, and *I did*, leaving my lovely home and my very important rezpondabilities behind. But I ask you this *one teeny-tiny favour* and you won't help poor old Picklewitch. I am very disappointed in you, Jack, very disappointed indeed. You are not the friend I thought you were, oh-dear-oh-dear-indeed. WOT a fudgenut. WOT a fopdoodle. WOT a frazzler.'

Jack wasn't going to fall for one of her tantrums.

'I'm sorry, Picklewitch, but rules are rules and that is that.'

'*YOU! BOY!*' A furious voice rang down the beach. It was Professor Bright holding onto his hat as he marched along. His gowns flapped like a sail in the sea breeze and he was followed by an obedient trail of children. '**Where do you think you have been?**' shouted the professor. 'I quite clearly told you the rule was NOT to go out of sight of the flag! We've been looking for you for the last half an hour. We have been very worried. I am very disappointed in you, young man.'

'I'm really very sorry, sir,' stuttered Jack. 'We ... we lost track of time and, you see um ... well, Picklewitch ...'

But where Picklewitch had been only seconds ago, now there was just a set of boot prints in the sand. A loud squawk caused Jack to look up,

just in time to see a green-eyed seagull hovering above him. With a resounding splat, a protest poo landed right in the middle of his clipboard.

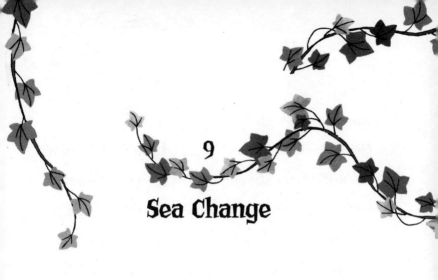

9

Sea Change

That night at dinner, Picklewitch's chair remained empty and Jack ate alone. This was probably just as well as he was in a stinker of a mood. *It's not fair*, he thought to himself, stabbing at his potatoes. He was doing his best – trying to follow the rules, working hard, recording all data like the greats that had gone before him, determined to unearth a ground-breaking fossil – and yet somehow here he was again, in trouble and on his own. *Why oh why* couldn't Picklewitch just be helpful for once? Behave reasonably? Do things in the right and proper way? Why couldn't she just enjoy the holiday and learn important scientific facts, not run off and get up to nonsense with her weird magic friends? Anyway, last time he checked, wizards were supposed to be men. And Scowling Margaret was definitely a woman. Then he remembered that Archie Cuckoo was a boy witch. Honestly, it was almost as if these people enjoyed breaking the rules.

He picked up a spoonful of custard and slopped it back into the dish. *Also,* he thought, *friends do not poo on other friends, even if they can turn into a seagull.*

Ting ting ting! Professor Bright stood up and tapped his glass with his spoon to get everyone's attention. 'Children! After a day of searching the cliffs and beach, I believe we have an announcement. It would seem that an important discovery has been made by one of our very own pupils. Victoria, please come to the front and show it to Dr Sharptooth.'

Victoria? Jack thought of her sitting on the deckchair, reading the baking magazine. How could *she* have made a discovery already when he hadn't? That wasn't fair! Jack's heart sank as the room broke into applause. The day was going from bad to worse.

Victoria pushed her chair in neatly and trotted to the front, placing an object carefully in their host's palm.

'Well, well,' said Dr Sharptooth, inspecting it through a magnifying glass with her good eye. 'A fine example of an ammonite, being from the Jurassic period, Obtuscum Zone I'd say. Very good work indeed, Victoria. And all on your own? The rest of you will have to try hard to improve

on this! I'd say it was good enough to be sold in a shop.'

Victoria returned to her seat, smiling a smile so sweet it seemed to give off its own sickly gas.

The last scrap of Jack's appetite disappeared as he faced up to the distinct possibility that Victoria might win the signed Bonestar hammer. Feeling desperate, Jack thought back to the beach, back to Scowling Margaret and to the ammonite around her neck. Where had she found that? *She's a beach local,* he thought, *like the great Mary Anning herself. She must know the best places to look. Surely it wouldn't hurt to ask?*

As if reading his mind, Picklewitch slipped, shadow-like, into the chair next to him and immediately tucked into his abandoned bowl of custard. 'Victoria's showing off, is she?' she slurped. 'Wot cheating skills she has! Very impressive. I spied her buying that fizzle in a shop in the high street.'

Jack looked over at Victoria, who was stroking her fossil, and felt the knot in his stomach tighten. NO. NO. NO. He would *not* let Victoria steal the glory, especially like this.

Picklewitch gave Jack a sly sideways glance. 'So, Jack. Mayhaps you're ready to change your mind about our little tea party invitation?'

'Well ...' Jack turned to Picklewitch, bit his lip and said, 'I suppose you don't get to visit a Sea Wizard's cave every day, do you? It might be very educational.'

'I KNEW it!' Picklewitch grinned and shovelled down the last scraps of his pudding. 'You is my best friend and the kipper's knickers too, Jack! We is the best team ever! Midnight picnic here we come!'

'Shh!' hissed Jack, looking around. 'Someone

will hear. Do you *absolutely promise* that nothing will go wrong this time?' he whispered. 'Like when it all went bad with your cousin, Archie Cuckoo? Do you promise that it will just be tea and cake and chat then straight home to bed? No funny business?'

With gusto, Picklewitch wiped the custard from her face. Then she pressed her hands together, put on her most angelic expression and said, 'Of course. Cross my heart and hope to fly.'

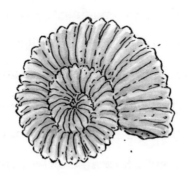

10

Moonlight Flit

It was much easier to sneak out of Draconis Hall that night than Jack had expected. He crept silently downstairs, past the library door, out of the dining hall and past the office window. His vivid imagination had created at least a dozen different ways he might be caught – creaking stairs, squeaking floorboards, locked doors, teachers having a late-night glass of water – all of which nearly made him change his mind. He spent quite a long time concocting a wildly unconvincing sleepwalking story and a grovelling apology, just in case he was spotted. But everyone was fast asleep and popping out into the darkness was actually as easy as shelling a pea.

Picklewitch waited for Jack at the end of the driveway and together they walked down the coast path to the shoreline. All the colours of the day had been washed away by the moon and now everything glittered a pale silver. This was what Picklewitch liked to call 'the thirteen o'clock of colours' on account of how useful it was in spells. Jack had been worried that he might be scared of the dark, so he brought his torch along, just in case. But somehow, with Picklewitch by his side, he didn't feel frightened at all. With hardly any other sound than the occasional whoosh and swoosh of the waves, it was as if the deserted beach belonged to them alone. He made a mental note to do more night exploration when he became a famous adventurer.

'Picklewitch, I've been wondering,' said Jack, crunching along the sand. 'Why is Scowling

Margaret so old? You and your cousin Archie Cuckoo are just children. Why is she different?'

'Most witches age like forests,' said Picklewitch, a faraway look in her eye. 'Slow and whispery. But Sea Wizards are even older – like the waves. It's rare to see them at all.'

Jack stopped and asked her a question that he knew she wouldn't answer. 'How old are *you*, Picklewitch?'

'Goodness, such a very nosy boy,' muttered Picklewitch briskly, picking up pace. 'With such very rude questions. Come on, you'll have to walk faster than that if you're going to keep up.'

Picklewitch took out her binoculars and inspected the silver sea. 'Aha, there it is,' she said. 'Right on time too. Come on.' They walked down to the shoreline together. A glass bottle was gently bobbing about on the waves, getting closer and closer. Picklewitch waded into the water and scooped it up in her hat.

'Is that a message in a bottle?' said Jack, finding it hard to contain his excitement. 'I've always wanted to find one of those!'

Picklewitch pulled the cork out with her teeth *POP* and wiggled a scroll of paper out with her finger. She unfurled it and scanned it quickly, nose to paper, muttering to herself.

'What does it say?' asked Jack over her shoulder, trying to see. 'Is it a map? A letter?'

Picklewitch handed the message over to Jack, squinted at the moon and picked up her pace. Like a sniffer dog, she began to criss-cross the beach, to and fro, back and forth, combing it for clues.

Jack looked at the message and read it aloud.

Seashore drift nor'-by-nor'west
Widdershins-widdershins salt
Slipper limpet spin deasil
Skywest and crooked
Samphire starboard
Stingwinkle south
mackerel moon
Northy starfish
Snakestone
Hinge
STOP
KNOCK LOUD 3 TIMES
DOORBELL'S BROKE

Scowling Margaret

'What does it mean?' said Jack.

'It's a Treasure Triangle, of course. Thought you was supposed to be clever? You didn't think she'd make it easy for us, did you?' called Picklewitch, zipping up and down, searching as she went. 'It'll lead us to the Sea Wizard's cave. Come on! Mustn't be late.'

Jack put the note into his pocket for safe keeping and chased after Picklewitch as she sprinted down the beach. How did she unpuzzle such strange clues so quickly, but not know what a fossil or a holiday was? Sometimes she seemed to know nearly nothing, and other times she was as cunning as a fox with a calculator.

It wasn't long before the sand beneath their feet changed to pebbly shale and then to smooth silvery rock. 'I know where we are,' cried Jack, looking down in wonder at the patterns beneath their feet.

'I've read about this place in *Fabulous Fossils*. This is the Ammonite Pavement! It's millions of years old! You can only see it when the tide is out.' Before them lay dozens of ammonite fossils fixed in the rock; some small, some large, some bold and some faint like moonlit ghosts.

Picklewitch skipped among the stones, racing back and forth. Every so often she stopped to taste the air and mutter the instructions to herself: '*Samphire starboard . . . Stingwinkle south . . . mackerel moon . . . northy starfish . . . snakestone . . .*' Eventually she spun on her heel and pointed straight down to the ground. '*Hinge. Aha. We has arrived.*'

Beneath her boot, embedded in the rock, lay a large ammonite the size of a bin lid. As Jack looked, he noticed a rusty iron hinge on its side, eroded by the sea. He wrinkled his brow. It looked just like a submarine hatch.

Picklewitch stamped her boot hard on the fossil hatch three times: *KNOCK KNOCK KNOCK*. 'OI! Scowling Margaret!' she shouted gleefully, standing back from the ammonite door. 'Is you in? It's me, Picklewitch, who has come for a lovely tea party in your beautifulest home.' She looked up at the moon and added, 'And I'm right on time too, so none of your nonsense, thank you.'

For a long minute, nothing happened. Then came the squish and slosh of wet boots, getting closer and closer, louder and louder. The ammonite lid creaked open on its hinge and Scowling Margaret's face popped out of the hole. She looked about as happy as a bulldog chewing a wasp.

'Oh, it's you. You'd better come in then, I s'pose,' she sniffed, looking them up and down. 'Wipe yer feet.'

The Sea Wizard turned and squelched back
down the corridor as Picklewitch stepped through
the hatch. Jack followed, feeling cautiously
around with his foot for the slippery steps. As
he descended down into the darkness, he had a
feeling that this might have been a bad idea.

11

Rock Cakes

Long, narrow and deep, the corridor was lit with a single stubby candle. It was dark and drippy and smelled of unmentionable things.

Picklewitch squealed, pointing up at the roof of the cave. 'Oh look!' she cried in delight at the hundreds of bats swinging back and forth. 'Party bunting! How pretty.'

'Picklewitch,' whispered Jack, his earlier bravado deserting him. 'I don't like this. It smells horrible and everything is damp and dark and it's the

middle of the night. I've changed my mind. Please can we go?'

'No we cannot,' hissed Picklewitch. 'I'm here for cake and I'm not leaving without it and that's that.'

The corridor opened up into a larger underground cavern where it was very difficult to see anything at all. Picklewitch and Jack groped around in the gloom for somewhere to sit.

After a few seconds Scowling Margaret appeared again, this time carrying a tray, rattling with teacups and a plate. She balanced the tray precariously on a rock and took a knife out of her pocket. After wiping it on her mackintosh, she sawed into the cake with some difficulty.

'What a smart sea cave you have 'ere, Margaret,' said Picklewitch, her greedy eye fixed on the cake. 'Have you lived here long?'

'None of yer business,' muttered Margaret,

plonking the slices of cake on tea plates.

Picklewitch persisted. 'Such lovely weather for the time of year, don't you think?'

The Sea Wizard humphed and thrust the plate at her.

'Oh my!' cried Picklewitch, wide-eyed in in mock surprise. 'For me? How most *terribly generous* of you, Scowling Margaret. You really is the most perfect host.' Picklewitch lifted the cake to her lips, opened her mouth wide and took a big bite. 'Ow, my gums!' she grumbled, her teeth rattling. 'It's as hard as rock and all salty-tasting too. Oi, Sea Wizard, how old is this 'ere fruitcake?'

Margaret shrugged. 'Got it from a shipwreck, maybe Elizabethan. I calls it my Disaster Cake.' She looked pointedly at Jack. 'S'pose your sad Boxie pet wants some too, does he?'

Jack looked alarmed. 'Oh no, thank you very much, Scowling Margaret.'

'Suit yourself. Don't want it going to waste,' she said, picking up the tray and shuffling back into the darkness.

'Well!' whispered Picklewitch behind her back. 'What a frazzling fudgenut, eh? A proper old mugswoggler and a hobbledehoy *she* is. Call that cake? More like one of your fossil fizzles than a delicious snack. I shall be sure to give her cave a very poor review in my Grimoire.' She pulled the grubby book out of her rucksack and began to scribble away.

Scowling Margaret's Sea Cave.
Stinks of grump.
No wind. Also technically indoors.
Cake hard enough to break a
badger's gnashers.

She put away her stubby pencil. 'I had such high hopes too, what with her being a Sea Wizard. Mayhaps a smidgeon of sea sponge or a little seaweed slice. At the very least a teeny-tiny blackberry tart.' She stuck out her bottom lip and made a sad face at Jack, fishing for extra sympathy. 'You know how much Picklewitch likes those.'

Scowling Margaret returned and they sat together in prickly silence. As Jack's eyes became more accustomed to the gloom, he could just about see that the Sea Wizard was sitting in a sort-of high-backed throne, seemingly carved out of the rock. The minutes passed like hours.

'Goodness me, Scowling Margaret, is that the time?' said Picklewitch, suddenly getting to her feet, much to Jack's relief. 'Thank you for such a warm and special welcome. However, as whizz-cracking as it's been, we must be on our way.'

Margaret pulled out a clay pipe and stuffed it with seaweed. 'What a pleasure it has been to welcome a visiting witch and her Boxie pet,' she muttered flatly. 'How the time does fly when you're having fun. Don't let me keep you, don't tell no one you saw me and don't never come back.' She pulled out a match, struck it on the rock and lit

her pipe. As she did so, the bright flash from the flame lit up the cave. And what Jack saw caused him to cry out loud.

12

Fossils and Fairytales

In that single blaze of the match, Jack had his first clear view of Scowling Margaret's throne. Her elbows were perched on huge bones and her feet rested upon enormous claws. Curled around the back was a long spinal column, which ended in a large skull the size of his suitcase. Halfway down the ribs were bones that looked like enormous broken umbrellas.

Excited, Jack fumbled for the torch in his pocket. He clicked the button and shone its narrow bright beam straight at the skeleton, running it over the

bones like a xylophone. Jack thought about his many reference books, sat at home on his bedroom shelf. *Could this really be what he thought it was?*

'Scowling Margaret,' he stuttered. 'I think you are sitting on ... on a ... on a ... ON A DINOSAUR FOSSIL!'

Jack had expected the two of them to be shocked or at the very least surprised. What he didn't expect was laughter.

'Did you hear that, Scowling Margaret?' sniggered Picklewitch. 'He thinks it's a dinosaur fossil!'

The Sea Wizard managed a tiny smirk, as if her face had never done it before. 'That is hilarious,' she said. 'Your pet is most amusing, ha ha.'

'It's not a joke!' protested Jack, becoming very animated. 'This is probably the most important find of the century!' He ran his hands over the skeletal remains. 'And it's complete! Do you have any idea how incredibly rare this is? It could possibly be some sort of Spinosaur, or maybe an Ichthyosaur!'

By now Picklewitch was full-on giggling, clutching at her sides.

'Picklewitch, stop it. This isn't funny,' said Jack, searching in his pockets for a pencil. 'I must record the evidence in my journal.'

'Oh, but it IS funny,' tittered Picklewitch.

Jack felt very annoyed. She should be squealing with delight and wonder. 'This is the greatest moment of my life and certainly no laughing matter. Could you please explain what's so funny?'

Picklewitch managed to compose herself. 'Certainly. I am laughing because any witch could tell you it's not a dinosaur.'

'Really?' said Jack, his hands on his hips and his

voice starting to sound very high-pitched. 'So what IS it then, seeing as you're such an expert?'

Picklewitch grinned and folded her arms. 'Shall we tell him, Margaret?'

Scowling Margaret got very close to Jack, inspecting him for signs of treachery. 'Is it a blabbermouth? 'Cos I like blabbermouths even less than Boxies.'

'Well, he's a fusspot and a fopdoodle all right,' said Picklewitch with a grin. 'But you can trust him.'

Scowling Margaret sparked another match, this time to light an enormous candelabra hanging from the cave roof. She lit all the candles, one by one, and the cavern gradually sprang into colour. As the gloom was banished into the corners, bright cave paintings emerged from the shadows. There were scenes of deserts, of the ocean, of fields and woods and mountains. In each were familiar beasts of red and green and blue. In some they were flying, in others they were breathing fire.

'No, NO!' cried Jack, shaking his head. 'I'm afraid you've made an error. These paintings are of *dragons*. Dragons aren't real, they are just made up. You see,' he said, always ready to explain, 'in evolutionary terms, dragons are not possible. Fire-breathing flying beasts with enormous bodies is silly. Any scientist will tell you this, it's just a fact.'

Picklewitch and Margaret looked at each other and smirked some more.

'Dragons are just fairytale fantasies,' Jack continued. 'They probably arose from ancient people finding fossils and not knowing what they were. And anyway, if dragons were real then there would be other skeletons around all over the place, wouldn't there?' He waved his arms around and toppled backwards, falling on another big pile of bones. 'There would be dragons everywhere!'

Margaret sighed and gently lifted her hat. Balanced snugly in the foamy white nest of her hair were a clutch of orbs, the size of a teacups.

'Are those ... *eggs?*' gasped Jack, his jaw hanging open.

'Told you you'd be glad you came, didn't I, Jack?' said Picklewitch, looking very pleased with herself.

'Well ... yes ... but if you think I'm going to believe ...' said Jack, pointing at Margaret and still very much determined to make his point, 'that she is some sort of *dragon babysitter,* you are very much mistaken. I don't want to disappoint you, but those are clearly fossilised dinosaur eggs that are millions of years old. I've seen them in the Natural History Museum. They certainly won't hatch.' Jack shook his head and thought for the hundredth time that witches would benefit from reading more books. 'I'm afraid I'd need a lot more evidence before I believe in dragons.'

Scowling Margaret looked very hard at Jack, then at Picklewitch. 'Your pet needs learning.' She lifted her necklace ammonite up to her lips and blew into it. A low whistle danced down the cave; a ribbon of watery sound. For a moment there was nothing. Then came a whoosh of flapping wings and an ear-splitting screech – a mighty cockerel's crow.

13

The Sea Wizard's Secret

To Jack's utter astonishment, an enormous beast strutted out of the darkest recesses of the cave, scratching, flapping and banging.

Picklewitch walked around the creature, making admiring noises. 'Well, well, Scowling Margaret, that's a fancy dragon and no mistake. A cockatrice, isn't it? I does approve of birdy-beings as you know and this is a fine and rare one indeed.'

'Don't make no sudden moves or loud noises though,' warned Scowling Margaret, sucking at her pipe. 'He don't like strangers.'

Jack stood as stiff as a board, immobilised by shock, barely able to believe his eyes. The dragon towered over him, his wings magnificently feathered in brilliantly vivid hues. His deep breast and thick, spiny tail were covered in copper scales that shimmered like coins in the candlelight. Jack couldn't help noticing the powerful feet, tipped with savage-looking claws, the heel spiked with a vicious spur. On the dragon's head was a leather hood, like those on birds of prey that Jack had seen in medieval films. A hooked golden beak and a blood-red cockerel comb peeked out of the holes. 'What's that for?' he stuttered, pointing a trembling finger.

"Tis a precaution,' said Scowling Margaret. 'Keeps him calm. One glance from a cockatrice and you'll be turned to stone.'

'Not everyone though,' said Picklewitch

knowingly, wagging her finger. 'As you know full well, Sea Wizard.'

Margaret straightened the eggs in her hair and pretended she hadn't heard.

Entranced by its strange beauty, Jack found himself slowly reaching out a hand to touch the cockatrice's feathers. They were soft and silken and through them he could feel the warmth of its body. As it leaned into him, Jack was enveloped in a delicious scent of toffee apples and fireworks. A low sound, somewhere between a cluck and a purr, began to vibrate all the way up from its chest and, to Jack's amazement, he realised the dragon's heart was beating in time with his own.

'For a beast not fond of strangers,' winked Picklewitch, 'he don't half like my boy.'

In this one magical moment, something between Jack and the cockatrice clicked. Normally anxious about everything from odd socks to bus timetables, Jack felt completely at home stroking this wild dragon. The feeling of trust was overwhelming and Jack couldn't explain it – but then nothing he was experiencing that night in the cave made any sense. One thing was certain though: Jack couldn't deny that this creature – *this mythical beast* – was as alive as he was.

As Jack struggled with the logic of the situation, the cockatrice puffed out its chest and stretched its magnificent rainbow wings, feather by feather. A blizzard of fluff rose up into the air and the down drifted, settling on the group like rainbow snowflakes. As one landed on Jack's nose, a tickle began in his nostrils. He desperately tried to keep still and quiet. *Oh no, please not now*, he thought, wriggling his nose to try and stop the impending sneeze. But it was too late!

'AAAATTCHOO!'

Startled by the sudden explosion, the cockatrice squawked and leapt backwards. A roar of orange fire belched from its beak and shot down the cave as if from a flamethrower.

'OI, wotch out,' shouted Picklewitch, patting her head furiously. 'That scorched my hat!'

'Be careful!' complained Scowling Margaret, waving plumes of smoke out of the way. 'Cockatrices is gentle, sweet souls and easily frighted.' She soothed the creature with little cooing noises, leading it back into the middle of the cave. 'Hush now, poor little thing, now-now, there-there. Margaret's here.' She tickled the dragon under its beak until it began to purr happily once more.

'This place is incredible,' breathed Jack, spinning around, trying to make sense of what he was seeing. 'What a treasure trove! Not only are there dragon skeletons in this cave, but there are eggs and *a real, live one too!*'

Hurriedly he pulled his journal and a pencil out of his back pocket. Picklewitch frowned. 'What do you think you're doing with that?' she asked.

'I'm recording the primary evidence, of course!' said Jack, his eyes bright with ambition. 'We must tell the world of this amazing discovery straight away!'

In unison, both Picklewitch and Scowling Margaret swung the full force of their mighty glares on Jack. Suddenly he could barely breathe. It felt like he was being crushed between the green of the woods and the blue of the sea.

'LISTEN TO ME, BOY,' bellowed Margaret. 'This place is **A SECRET**. I've kept these dragons safe all my long, long life. YOU SHALL **NEVER**,' she said, stabbing a knobbly, wrinkled finger in his chest, 'SPEAK OF THIS **EVER TO NO ONE**.' She seemed to get bigger by candlelight, looming over him like an enormous wave. 'Because if you do, bad things will happen. Firstly I shall turn you into a crab. Then I'll make your teeth too big for your head. And THEN I'll make sure all your bones wobble for ever and a day. And that's just for starters . . .'

'Now, now, Margaret, everybody calm down. Don't get over-excited,' said Picklewitch, squeezing between them. 'He don't mean no harm. He's just a silly Boxie saying silly Boxie things. He won't breathe a word to a soul, will you, Jack?'

'But Picklewitch,' gasped Jack, not knowing when to shut up, 'Dr Sharptooth must be told! Imagine how grateful she'll be. Remember what she said? That if we were to find something remarkable then we should tell her ... that a child might discover something remarkable ... and I have! This is the most incredible discovery ever!'

Scowling Margaret gave a hollow laugh. 'Pah! The Sharptooths? Rotten to the core, maggots at heart. Always have been, always will be. Cheaters, thieves and robbers – one and all!'

Jack frowned. 'How can you say that? You're wrong!' he protested. 'Dr Firenza Sharptooth is *a world-class fossil expert*. I've never even heard her mention anything about dragons! On top of this she is extremely clever and a good person.

She's my hero.'

'Listen to me, foolish boy, and listen well,' spat Margaret, so close to Jack that he could see the veins in her eyes. 'The Sharptooths aren't interested in fossils. The Sharptooths are dragon hunters. They've been desperate to find this cave for centuries.'

Scowling Margaret sunk back down into her fossil throne. 'Year on year I sees them searching along the beach, hammers and brushes and books, all the time sneaking and peeking. But I protects my dragons from harm and that is how it's going to stay. We're safe here, tucked away beneath the ammonites.' She lit her pipe. 'Now, are you going to solemnly swear to keep this a secret or do I have to curse you to an eternity of jiggling sideways down the seashore, all made of jelly with teeth the size of shoes?'

14

Cockcrow Alarm

As they wandered back home along the beach, Picklewitch tried to explain. 'See, there's all sorts of magical folk. Tree Witches like me look after the birds and the butterflies and the hedgehogs. Archie Cuckoo was a Wyrd, so he was just a good-for-nothing fudgenut. A Sea Wizard's job is to look after the dragons, from when they are little eggs to a pile of dusty old bones. Wizards and dragons go together like thunder and lightning, or the stars and the moon.'

'Well, she doesn't have to be so horrible about Dr Sharptooth,' said Jack, still smarting at the injustice. 'If Margaret met her she'd know how wrong she is. She's totally got the wrong end of the stick. Dragon hunters? What nonsense. The Sharptooths are fossilists, plain and simple.'

'If you say so,' said Picklewitch, finding an old cake paper in her pocket. She gave it a lick. 'But I wouldn't be so sure.'

As they reached Draconis Hall, Picklewitch leapt up onto the garden wall. '*Remember, Jack –* no matter what you think, you saw **nothing** and you heard **nothing** and you know **nothing** about **nothing**. The dragons must stay secret. Never cross a Sea Wizard.' Then she slipped into the trees and was gone.

Jack tutted and shook his head. For as long as he could remember he'd dreamed of making a really big scientific discovery and sharing it with the world. Tonight his dream had finally come true but now he had to keep it a secret! Typical. This holiday was turning out not at all how he had expected. He looked up to see the bright moon illuminating the gargoyles perched on the guttering and shivered. It was cold and late. Time for bed.

Jack slipped inside and closed the front door quietly behind him. The hallway was silent, but for the ticking of a grandfather clock. It said half past three in the morning and Jack realised that he would only get four hours' sleep before breakfast. He had run out of time to find a fossil so there was no chance of winning the Bonestar hammer now.

But it didn't really matter. Compared with that night's remarkable events, the prize didn't feel that important any more. He would just have to settle for meeting a real live dragon instead. Jack sniffed his jumper – it still carried a tell-tale trace of toffee apples and fireworks. Grinning to himself, he tiptoed through the dining hall and placed his foot on the bottom stair, ready to creep back up to the dorms.

For the first time Jack noticed the PRIVATE sign on the library door, the one that Dr Sharptooth had used to make such a dramatic entrance on the first morning. *Aren't libraries supposed to be open to everybody?* he thought. Despite it being the middle of the night, a pool of light leaked out from beneath the closed door. *Who could be in there at this late hour?* Full of curiosity, Jack reached out and turned the brass doorknob, but it didn't open.

He bent down and squinted through the keyhole but couldn't see anything. *Was it locked from the inside?* He pressed his ear to the door. There was a faint and mysterious rumbling.

Jack noticed a newspaper on a side table and remembered an old trick. Would it work? Feeling bold after his midnight adventure, he peeled off one sheet from the newspaper and slid it silently through the gap under the door. Then he took out his pencil and poked and prodded at the key until it fell out and landed on the newspaper with a small *clank*. Slowly and carefully Jack tugged at the newspaper and pulled it back out under the door, along with the key.

Wide awake and holding his breath, Jack inserted the iron key into the hole and turned it. With only the slightest pressure, the door swung open.

In the far corner of the room a figure lay slumped over a desk, softly snoring. Jack recognised her straight away; it was the great Dr Firenza Sharptooth herself, asleep in the lamplight on top of an open book. His heart immediately softened. Here was this great academic mind, studying into the small hours of the morning and so devoted to her studies that she hadn't made it to bed, all in the name of scientific research. He shook his head. How dare Scowling Margaret say those things about the Sharptooths? It was completely unfair. Oh, how Jack *wished* he could tell Firenza about the dragon and the cave; she would be so excited. But a promise was a promise.

Jack was about to back out of the door again when his eye was drawn to the library shelves. Temptation tickled; surely this must be one of the best reference libraries on fossils in the world.

Could it do any harm to have a quick peek?

Carefully, Jack took down a scroll of parchment and unravelled it to reveal an illuminated manuscript. Dated 1342, it was an illustration of a long-bodied creature called the Lambton Worm. He took down another; this time a picture of St George and the dragon, locked in battle with fire and blades. As Jack explored further he came across dozens upon dozens of books all about British dragons: Knuckers, wyverns and wyrms. There were plenty on the other shelves too, only these were about dragons in other lands – the Yong of China, the Tiamat of Syria, the Wawel of Poland, the Coca of Portugal.

Where are the books on fossils? wondered Jack, working his way across the shelves, a sense of panic rising in his chest. *Why are all these texts about dragons?*

Jack took down a notebook, this time a Victorian diary. It had the name 'Dr Charles Sharptooth' embossed in gold on the brown leather cover. He undid the clasp and read the first page:

Sunday 23rd October 1898

Dear Diary,

To my great joy, I have heard yet more whispers of dragons in Dorset— this time a cockatrice nest! My informers say there is an underground cave, hidden somewhere along the shoreline.

Jack clamped his hand over his mouth to stop a gasp escaping.

Word is that, as usual, it's protected by magic. To this end I have decided to purchase a property near the cliffs, which I intend to name Draconis Hall. Here I can work unhindered, disguised as a fossilist; it's all the fashion these days. The work will be dangerous as cockatrices are known for their nasty natures. But I must have one— dead or alive.

Jack's eyes were drawn to a framed, embroidered sampler on the wall.

The lion lies down with the lamb,
and the child, if it will,
may harmlessly put its hand
into the cockatrice's den.

The Spell of Egypt, 1908

Next to it was a scrap of medieval tapestry. It featured a young boy, hand-feeding a feathered dragon and stroking its head.

Jack's brain began to whirr as all the pieces fell into place: the private library, the books, the setting, the locked door.

Of course – *Draconis* was Latin for dragon! Jack thought back to the gargoyles on the roof. They were all dragons too. He looked closely again at the scrap of tapestry. Was this why Firenza Sharptooth invited pupils of St Immaculate's here to search the shoreline? Because only a *child* can befriend a cockatrice?

It was then that Jack's eye fell on a letter lying next to Dr Sharptooth. He crept over and read it.

Dear Major General Cavendish-Jones
(War Office)
Re: Codename Cockcrow

As I have already explained, a cockatrice can both breathe fire and turn the enemy to stone in a single glance. Add to this their power, savagery and ability to fly, they are the **ultimate weapon of war**. The price on its head is eighty million pounds which, I'm sure you will agree, is fair.

Progress is slow, but I have teams of gifted children searching the shoreline. I feel certain that a breakthrough will be made and a live specimen will be caught any day now.

Yours,
Dr Firenza Sharptooth
Dragon Hunter

Bitter betrayal washed over Jack as his worst fears were confirmed. What a fool he had been. All this time he had thought she was a proper scientist but really she was no better than a Big Game hunter. All that mattered to her was money, not knowledge. And to think he had wanted to tell her all about it! Tears pricked the back of his eyes as he imagined his gentle friend being used as a weapon. Jack remembered the soft warmth of the dragon's feathers, how frightened it had been of a mere sneeze.

Jack frowned and clenched his fists in anger. How could she? The dragons must be protected. Dr Sharptooth must *never* find the cave. No wild creature should ever be used in this way, especially not something as rare and beautiful as the cockatrice. One thing was for sure – Jack's lips were sealed. He would *never-ever-ever* tell anyone where the dragons were, even if it meant giving up on the dream of having his name on a brass plaque in the Natural History Museum. Some things were more important than scientific fame. Glory was one thing, but friendship was another matter entirely. It was time to pack up, go home and leave the dragons in peace.

Jack silently backed out of the library and pulled the door shut behind him. He crept up the stairs, his face full of frowns. A stupid signed hammer as a prize? The price of betrayal? No thank you. Jack didn't want anything with the Sharptooth name on it, even if it were the last fossil hammer in the world. Victoria was welcome to it.

15

Triangle of Trouble

A couple of hours later Jack awoke to find Aamir tapping him on the shoulder. 'Jack,' he whispered. 'Quickly – you need to get up. You've overslept and missed breakfast! Dr Sharptooth wants to see you in her office.'

Jack groggily pulled on his clothes, wishing he'd set his alarm. He had only slipped into bed as the sun came up and felt very tired indeed.

He went downstairs and knocked on the office door. A voice said, 'Enter. Please shut the door behind you.'

Dr Firenza Sharptooth was sitting at the desk and next to her stood Victoria, as smug as a cat with a saucer of cream. What was *she* doing here?

'Ah, Jack, thank you for coming. I'm afraid it's bad news. Victoria has told me you have broken the rules. How disappointing.'

As Firenza Sharptooth was no longer his hero, Jack didn't feel as sorry as he might. 'Victoria is always trying to get me in trouble,' he said, unable to hold in his yawns. 'Is this about me oversleeping? Or is it about wandering out of sight of the flag yesterday? Because I've already apologised for that.'

'It's a lot worse than that!' crowed Victoria, pointing her finger. 'I saw you! You and Picklewitch, sneaking off together into the night like a pair of thieves.'

Oh no. Jack felt his blood turn to ice. He had

been so careful, *so sure* no one had seen them.

'I followed you,' said Victoria, wagging her finger, 'right down to the seashore. I saw that *witch* take a message out of a bottle and then I watched *you* put it in your pocket.'

Jack tried to force a laugh, but it came out as a strangled squawk. 'Don't be so silly, Victoria,' he said. 'What a vivid imagination you have. You've probably eaten too many muffins and had a bad dream, that's all. They are bad for the digestion, you know. I've been asleep all night, tucked up in my bunk bed.'

'*Really?*' said Dr Sharptooth, inspecting Jack's expression very closely with her one eye. 'You won't mind us looking in your pocket then, will you?'

'What?'

'Your pocket,' she repeated in clipped tones. 'I should like to see what is in it.'

The whole world seemed to stand still. Jack inched his fingers into his pocket, hoping for all the world that the note had blown away, that he had somehow misplaced it or that maybe a seagull had stolen it. But there it was, safe and sound, a small scroll curling beneath his fingertips.

'RIGHT NOW, PLEASE,' insisted Dr Sharptooth, holding out her hand.

Jack's emotions were in turmoil, but he had no choice but to hand it over. As Dr Sharptooth unfurled it, her one eye glittered in anticipation. 'This is a Treasure Triangle,' she murmured 'I never thought I would see one of these.' She sniffed at it suspiciously before her glance snapped back up at Jack. 'Do you know what these words mean?'

'I know! I know! I think it's a sort of map!' cried Victoria, overcome with the need to spill the beans. 'It led them to a door in the floor. A big, round fossil door!'

Jack wanted to push Victoria into a cupboard and slam it shut. What a blabbermouth!

Firenza Sharptooth was now on her feet, holding Victoria's arms by her side in a fierce grip. '*Where* was this door?' she demanded, speaking in slow and deliberate tones. '*Tell me now, child.*'

Victoria's smug face now looked a little frightened and she twisted to get out of the hold. 'It's . . . it's down on the beach. After they went into the hole I got scared on my own. Then I got lost . . . so I couldn't say for certain where it was. Fossils all look alike to me. It was a big, flat bit of rock with lots of stone spirals in it. What more do you need to know? The point is they broke the rules! Could you let go please? That hurts.'

'Useless idiot!' spat Firenza, pushing Victoria aside. 'I shall just have to make the boy show me where it is then.' She turned to speak to Jack, but the room was empty. He was long gone.

Jack skidded down the corridor and ran out of the front door as fast as his legs would take him. He had to find Picklewitch and warn Scowling Margaret!

'PICKLEWITCH! PICKLEWITCH!' he cried as he pelted through the grounds. 'HELP! HELP!'

'SHH!' Picklewitch grabbed him and pulled him down into a large shrub. 'Come down here!'

'Oh, Picklewitch,

thank goodness!' whimpered Jack, crouching down next to her, his words spilling over each other. 'The Sea Wizard was right – about the Sharptooths, about the dragons, about everything!'

'Yes, well,' said Picklewitch, looking furtively around, 'witches ain't as daft as Boxies, you know.'

'Yes, yes, and I'm really, really sorry. But now something terrible has happened and it's all my fault!' Jack tried his best to hold in the tears, but he was tired and frightened and angry all at once.

Picklewitch put a stiff arm around him, as if this sort of thing didn't come naturally to her. 'There, there, stop yer wailing, I knows all about it anyway.'

'Do you? But how?' snuffled Jack

She rolled her eyes. 'Because I'm a witch, aren't I, you daft fudgenut?'

From beneath the shrub, they watched Firenza

march past, crunching across the gravel and heading down the cliff path to the beach.

'Oh no!' whispered Jack. 'She's going to use the Treasure Triangle to find them herself!'

'Not if we gets there first.' Picklewitch took her Grim out of her rucksack and began to flick through the pages. 'Now, pull yerself together. There's no time to waste. This calls for some emergency magic.'

16

Flights of Fancy

'What are you looking for?' whispered Jack, as Picklewitch scrabbled through the pages of her Grim.

'A travel spell for two.'

'For two? But ... other than the protection umbrella spell, you've never done any magic on me.' Jack looked worried. 'Will it hurt?'

'Mayhaps,' muttered Picklewitch, still searching. 'A bit.'

'Picklewitch, I'm not sure about ...'

'AHA!' Picklewitch stabbed at the page with her

finger, ignoring his protests. 'Here it is on Page 32.' She took a bottle of homemade walnut ink from her pocket and poured it in a sploshy circle on the driveway. In the centre she marked an X with two crossed twigs. Then she pulled the end of a pink fishing net out of her rucksack and put it on top. It was interlaced with long strands of seaweed and clearly rescued from a bin.

Jack stared at it gloomily, unsure how all this was going to help.

'Excellent,' said Picklewitch, clapping her hands. 'I duz love a bit of recycling.' Then, closing her eyes, she began to whisper to herself.

Magic tandem transformation
Squawker-shrieker transportation
Icy I-screams and saucy pot
Now this X marks the spot
Tiny witchy, Boxie brave
Tangled net - to the cave!

Out of the clouds burst a pair of seagulls, wheeling and reeling together in the blue sky. They hovered above Picklewitch and Jack, flapped, stuck out their yellow feet and came skidding to a halt on the dusty gravel.

Picklewitch looked at Jack and pointed at the pink plastic fishing net. 'Get in, then.'

If Jack hadn't felt so anxious he would have laughed. 'Get in? I can't possibly fit into that little ...'

Jack's protests were interrupted by a sudden

burp and a big bubble popped out of his mouth. Then he had a sensation of disappearing from the inside out, like the sand slipping away from the centre of an egg timer. His head filled with rose and lemon sparkles and, without warning, everything went black.

When Jack opened his eyes he was sitting in the middle of the pink fishing net, next to Picklewitch, looking up at a pair of enormous seagulls. To his great alarm, the birds seemed to have become the size of buses. He was about to tell Picklewitch that her spell had gone wrong when he realised the birds weren't big at all. It was *he and Picklewitch* that had shrunk and now they were as tiny as clothes pegs! Picklewitch handed him a pair of goggles.

'Wear these 'cos you is a only beginner.' She raised her little arms and, speaking in a tinny voice, she commanded, 'Birds! To the Sea

Wizard's cave ... and make it sharpish!'

The seagulls obediently picked up the fishing net in their beaks and took off into the air, swinging it like a hammock. 'Hold on, Jack,' giggled Picklewitch, her hands firmly gripping the brim of her hat and shouting above the wind. 'Or you'll be a fish supper! Tally ho!'

When the first scare had worn off, Jack began to enjoy the ride. The water glittered blue and silver, racing beneath them. He could see the white crests of waves and feel the sea breeze blasting against his goggles as they zoomed towards the shore. In only a couple of minutes they found themselves coming in to land on the Ammonite Pavement. 'But which one is the hatch?' fretted Jack, as they circled around and around. 'They all look so similar today.'

'That one there, of course,' said Picklewitch,

pointing. 'I'd know it anywhere. I thought you said you liked fossils? *Ding-ding! Next stop please.* We'll get off here, thank you, seagulls.'

The birds hovered above the hinged ammonite door and then lowered the net gently onto it. Picklewitch and Jack climbed out, two little windblown dolly pegs standing on a big rock.

Picklewitch looked Jack up and down and tutted. 'Well, this won't do at all.' She clicked both sets of fingers three times and said:

Megatronic
Wizard's den
Make us proper big again.

With a hiccup, a gulp and a fizz from top to toe, they were the right size once more. Picklewitch jumped up and down on the ammonite door, stamping her boots.

KNOCK KNOCK KNOCK

Stepping back, she cupped her hands and hollered, 'SEA WIZARD! 'Tis us, Picklewitch and Jack. Let us in!'

There was no answer.

'SCOWLING MARGARET, 'TIS I, YOUR GOOD FRIEND PICKLEWITCH.'

This time the hatch creaked open and Scowling Margaret's hatless head popped out, eggs nestled in her hair. She looked startled, as if she'd been caught in her pyjamas.

'What do you want? I've already wasted my best cake on you. Everyone knows the Code says only one visit. GO. AWAY.' She was about to slam the lid shut when Picklewitch leaned forward and whispered in the Sea Wizard's ear.

Margaret listened, all the while scowling so hard her eyebrows crossed like a pair of knitting needles. She tipped the cave lid wide open. 'S'pose you better come in then.'

17

Hatstand

The two of them followed the Sea Wizard down along the dripping corridor and into the glow of the candlelit cavern.

Scowling Margaret sat down on her throne and pulled a giant clamshell up onto her lap. Opening the palms of both hands, she began to chant:

Barnacles, sea bees
Fingers and teeth
Stars and water
Show the thief

Seawater began to gush from her fingertips, filling the clamshell, as light from the candelabra danced on its surface. When it was full to the brim, Margaret peered down at the quivering reflection. 'Aha. There she is. Have a look.'

Jack leaned over the edge of the shell. He could see Firenza Sharptooth in the water! She was desperately scouring the beach for clues, looking down at the Treasure Triangle in her hand, then up, then down again. Scowling Margaret leaned back and sighed. 'It's all right. She's going in the wrong direction. Anyway, only magic folk can read a Treasure Triangle. We're perfectly safe. No harm can come to us.'

Jack let out a big sigh of relief. 'I'm really very sorry I didn't believe you about Dr Sharptooth, Margaret,' he said, hanging his head in shame. 'I . . . I snuck into her private library and it was full of dragon books, barely a single one on fossils. Can you believe she was planning to sell the cockatrice as a weapon? She's not the person I thought she was at all.'

'There, there,' said the Sea Wizard, patting him on the head. 'You is only a silly Boxie pet – you can't be expected to know about anything important. At least you don't bite.'

Jack smiled to himself as the guilt ebbed away. 'Well, if everything's all right and the cave is safe, could I, possibly, *maybe* see the cockatrice again?' he asked hopefully. 'Like, *really* see him this time? Without the hood?' Picklewitch and Margaret exchanged warning glances. 'It's all right – I'm not worried,' said Jack, feeling brave once more. 'I know that he wants to be my friend.'

'Oh go on, Margaret,' cajoled Picklewitch. 'You know he's right. Don't be such an old misery guts.

We're going home today anyway.'

'Well ... he does have a soft spot for the boy, I s'pose. But this is the last time.' Reluctantly Margaret lifted the necklace ammonite to her lips and blew. The cockatrice bounded out straight away, delighted that Jack was back.

'Hello again, boy!' laughed Jack, stroking the silky rainbow feathers, reaching his arms around the creature's neck.

The cockatrice clucked and cooed as Jack carefully undid the leather laces at the back of the hood and slowly, gently slipped it off. The cockatrice blinked in the brightness of the candlelight, as his gaze settled on Jack. For an anxious moment, everyone held their breath. The dragon's blue eyes were like brilliant sapphires, their quicksilver centres flashing like mirror balls. He cocked his head first to one side, then the other. Finally the cockatrice put one golden-clawed foot forward and bowed graciously.

Jack bowed in return and then looked him straight in the eye. 'Nice to see you properly at last, mister cockatrice. It's an honour to be your friend.' He stroked the dragon's feathers and marvelled at its beauty. He wouldn't forget this magical moment as long as he lived and he never wanted it to end.

'*Hello?*' A horribly familiar voice echoed down the cave corridor. 'Is anyone there?'

Startled, the cockatrice shrank back into the shadows. Jack dropped the hood in shock.

Scowling Margaret sprang to her feet in alarm and the giant clamshell clattered to the floor, water spilling everywhere. 'Who goes there?' she hissed.

'You *did* shut the hatch, didn't you, Jack?' hissed Picklewitch, staring wide-eyed at Jack.

'ME?' exclaimed Jack. '*You* were last in! I thought **YOU** were supposed to be shutting the hatch!'

But it was too late to figure out who was to blame because there, in the entrance to the cave, stood Dr Firenza Sharptooth, lit up in the candlelight.

'I knew it! My great-great-grandfather was right. It is real!' she cried, whipping off her eye patch to get a better look. Both eyes glittering with excitement, she gazed around at the paintings on the wall, at the fossils and the bones. 'The old stories of the dragon cave are true after all!' She spotted Scowling Margaret and gasped. 'A Sea Wizard carrying eggs! LIVE EGGS!' Firenza Sharptooth laughed hysterically and twirled around, taking it all in. 'I can't believe it! My wildest dreams have come true at last! I told them, didn't I? But no one would believe me!' She raised both arms in victory. 'Well, NOW THEY WILL HAVE TO!'

Jack hoped and prayed that the cockatrice would stay in hiding, scared by the noise and safely tucked away in the depth of the cave. Then he had a clever idea – he would make an even bigger racket! That would be sure to keep him away.

'YOU ARE A TERRIBLE PERSON, FIRENZA SHARPTOOTH! EVEN YOUR EYE PATCH IS FAKE!' Jack yelled. 'YOU'RE A LIAR AND A THIEF AND A CHEAT!'

'He's right, you know, you really are,' said Picklewitch matter-of-factly, inspecting her nails. 'Have you ever considered becoming a witch?'

Noticing her for the first time, Dr Sharptooth cast a withering glance at Picklewitch. '*You*. You're the girl with the porridge in her trousers and the pointy hat. I knew from the first day there was something wrong with you.'

'It's very *rude* to make personal hobservations,' said Picklewitch, removing a winkle from her ear and polishing it on her dungarees.

'I SAID,' repeated Jack, rather annoyed that no one seemed to be paying any attention to his efforts, 'that YOU are a criminal who should be locked up. You used to be my hero. I thought you were a beautiful science-pirate but you turned out to be just a ... a ... plain old pirate! You and your stupid Bonestar competition! It was all a cover-up!'

he scrabbled for the worst insult he could think of: 'You are a ROTTEN SCIENTIST!'

'Boohoo,' smirked Firenza Sharptooth. 'As if I care what some silly little boy thinks. I'm going to be rich and that's all that matters.' She turned to Scowling Margaret, who had stayed surprisingly quiet throughout this whole exchange. 'Now, Sea Wizard: I demand that you surrender your cockatrice. Where is it?'

'Couldn't possibly say,' said Scowling Margaret, leaning forward. 'Maybe you would like one of these precious dragon eggs instead?' Dr Firenza Sharptooth's eyes sparkled with greed as they roved over the clutch in Margaret's hair.

'NO! Don't let her, Margaret!' cried Jack, horrified by the suggestion. 'She'll only use them to experiment on! Or breed them as dangerous weapons! You mustn't let her have any!'

'At last,' crooned Firenza, ignoring Jack and reaching out for the glowing orbs. 'Come here, my little baby dragons. Mummy Sharptooth will take care of you now.'

But the instant her fingers touched the eggs, a bloodcurdling shriek erupted from the back of the cave. Black, acrid smoke billowed into the candlelight as the enraged cockatrice came thundering like an armoured tank out of the shadows, screaming fire and fury. 'Boohoo again,' smirked Scowling Margaret.

For one brief and glorious second, her mouth caught in a perfect *O* of horror and

delight, the dragon hunter's eyes met the blazing glare of the cockatrice. Then, with a loud *crack* and *crick* and *crunch* Dr Firenza Sharptooth, fossil expert and best-selling author, turned to stone.

'Fancy that,' observed Picklewitch. 'She looks just like a fizzil herself now!' She inspected the stone figure closely. 'But once a stinkfungus,' she said, giving Firenza a sniff, 'always a stinkfungus.'

'All's well that ends well,' said Scowling Margaret, placing the hood back on the blinking cockatrice. 'Now if you don't mind,' she said, shooing Picklewitch and Jack towards the exit, 'I've really got to get on.'

'But ... just like that?' protested Jack, over his shoulder. 'I have to say a proper goodbye!'

Not waiting for permission, Jack pushed past the Sea Wizard and made a dash for it. He reached up and threw his arms around the cockatrice's neck, burying his face in its warm down and breathing in the smoky sweet scent. 'Goodbye, my friend,' he whispered. 'I wish we could have had more time together.' The dragon nuzzled his beak in Jack's hair and made a sad clucking sound. 'I'll never forget you, mister cockatrice.'

Scowling Margaret's expression softened for just a second, like the sun coming out from behind a cloud, before quickly disappearing again. Pulling herself together, she grabbed Jack firmly by the elbow and began to escort him from the premises.

'But what shall I tell everyone back at Draconis Hall?' he asked.

Scowling Margaret continued to push Jack and Picklewitch up the corridor and out of the hatch. 'Margaret,' demanded Jack, before she could slam it. 'What are you going to do with Dr Sharptooth?'

'Tree Witch, does your Boxie pet *ever* stop

asking questions? Bumbling barnacles, I don't knows hows you put up with it.' The Sea Wizard rolled her eyes and sighed. 'If you *must* know, I've been needing a new hatstand for a while and a Sharptooth will do the job nicely.' She gave them a final shove out into the light. 'Now, off you go, quickly quickly. No time to waste. Good riddance. Goodbye for ever.' With this she heaved the ammonite door shut and bolted it from the inside with *a clink, a clunk and a clank*. Faintly they could hear her parting words, flung over her shoulder, as she sloshed down the corridor. 'Time to go home.'

18

Epilogue

Back home at Rookery Heights, Jack pushed open the rickety wooden door. He could tell straight away that the garden was in a very good mood indeed. The leaves on the trees fluttered prettily and a paintbox of poppies, daisies and marigolds swayed in bliss around the edges of the paths. It was clearly very happy to have Picklewitch back where she belonged.

'Ah,' called Picklewitch, catching sight of him. 'There you are, Jack. I was just telling the story of *What I Did On My Holidays* again. You are just in

time to hear my lecture entitled *The Seaside*.' An attentive audience of sparrows, crows, magpies, pigeons and owls were lined up around the pond edge, ready for the next performance. Picklewitch was sitting in the middle of the pond, murky water up to her waist, once again wearing the saggy swimming costume from the museum. Despite Jack's insistence that she return it, Picklewitch had refused point blank.

'The seaside,' began Picklewitch, 'is full of strangeness, the likes of which you *has never seen*. There be peculiar salty winds and mists for a start. There's starfish and cushion stars and butterfish, I-screams, razor clams and singing winkles. The salty wind is most refreshing.' The pigeons cooed in wonder and the sparrows twittered excitedly. 'But,' Picklewitch sighed, 'overall I would have to say that the trees are too spiky, sand gets in uncomfortable places and that it's very wet at the edges.' She pulled a newt out of her swimming costume. 'It was interesting to meet a Sea Wizard, though her home was nowhere as beautifulishous as mine.' Her eyes narrowed as she recalled the meeting. 'And I must say the cake was of a very poor standard.'

'Ice creams and wetness? Winkles and cushion stars? Is that all?' laughed Jack. He took off his shoes and socks and lowered his feet into the cool green of the pond. 'Aren't you going to tell them about the *dragon*?'

Picklewitch closed her eyes and turned her face up to the sun. 'Dragon? What a strange thing to say, Jack. I'm sure I have no idea what you're talking about.'

Jack laughed, sploshing his feet in the pond. 'Ha ha. Very funny. You know – the eggs? The cave?

My friend the cockatrice?'

'What a colourful imagination you has for a Boxie,' she sniffed. 'Really though, you shouldn't spread such nonsense. Imagine if people started to believe in dragons! Very silly and unscientific. Everybody knows that dragons isn't real. They is only in stories.'

Jack's face fell. 'But ... but Picklewitch ... they *are* real! You saw it. We were there ...'

Picklewitch climbed out of the water and shook like a wet cat. 'That's better,' she said. 'Nice and cool now. No such thing as the wrong sort of weather you know, Jack, only the wrong sort of clothes.' She reached down into her rucksack. 'By the way, a seagull delivered this earlier. Got your name on it.'

She pulled out a big brown envelope. It was addressed:

Picklewitch's Boxie Pet
The Garden
Rookery Heights

As Jack carefully opened it up and reached inside, his fingertips brushed against something delicate and soft. As he pulled out a long feather, he could see it was the colours of the rainbow and edged with silver and gold.

'It's from Scowling Margaret!' he gasped. Jack held it up and it shimmered in the sunshine, sparkling with magic. 'This is SO MUCH better than a fossil hammer,' he grinned, stroking it in disbelief.

'From some exotic bird no doubt, maybe from the Hamazon,' said Picklewitch. 'Probably a Sunshine Plomper or a maybe Stardust CrackerJack. Definitely, certainly, *absolutely not* a dragon,' she winked heavily, 'should anyone ever ask.'

Picklewitch's tummy let out a loud rumble. 'I-screams is all very well,' she said, dragging a long strand of pondweed out of her matted hair, 'but they is not nearly as yumptious as Ladymum's raspberry slices.'

She looked around at the garden, up at her tree and then back at the house. 'You know, Jack, I don't think I shall be going on holiday again anytime soon. I think I'll leave all that giddy widdershins up to the birds.'

With this, Picklewitch skipped into the house, dripping pond water, lining the path with puddles and singing at the top of her voice:

'Sea lettuce PIE and STARfish FOAM
FIZ-zle FOSsil, mermaid's COMB
Wherever I may STRAY or ROAM
NOWHERE
IZ AZ
GOOD
AZ
HOME.'

THE END . . .

EXTRAS

THE JURASSIC JOURNAL NEWSPAPER

CLIFF-TOP DRAMA IN DORSET

Today, in a dramatic landslip, part of Draconis Hall, home to the Sharptooth family for generations, crumbled into the sea. During a mighty summer storm, a single, huge wave caused part of the cliff to fall away, taking the house with it. Recently Draconis Hall had hosted a school party, but fortunately on the day of the incident the house was empty and no one was hurt. On a positive note, the landslip did reveal the skeleton of a new species of dinosaur, which is due to be transported to the Natural History Museum in London.

When questioned, one local elderly woman said, 'You've never seen a wave like it. It was like something summoned up by an angry wizard. Now go away.'

The owner of the property, Dr Firenza Sharptooth, was unavailable for comment.

SPELL TO CALL THE NINTH WAVE

1 for a dragon
2 for a snitch
3 for a boy
4 for a witch
5 for a whistle
6 for the bold
7 for a secret
never to be told
8 for a wish
on sea wizard's frown,
to call the 9th wave
and bring the house down.

SWITCHY-WITCHY SEASONS SPELL

Flash of wind
Gust of ice
Flake of mist
Throw the dice
Leafy trees
Green to brown
Turn the summer
Upside down.

SPELL TO TURN A SEEGULL INTO A SOSSIDGE

Skwark and titter
Grey and white
Flip and flap
Burd in flite
Sizzle sozzle
Lishous bite
Har har har
Servz you rite

HANDY HINTS ON KEEPING YOUR SWIMMING COZZY CUMFY

1. Wash in rainy puddles.
2. Ask Stormbeest to run around with it in a warm wind.
3. Burds will mend holes with badger tummy fluff.
4. Warning: Never let hedgehogs sleep in it.

LIST OF PICKLEWITCH'S HOLIDAY SOUVENIRS

Shells
Pebbles
Driftwood
Top-of-the-range Bonestar
    fossil hammer

PICKLEWITCH'S FAVOURITE
I-SCREAMS IN ORDER:

Strawberry

Salted Caramel

Vanilla

Honeycomb

Raspberry Ripple

(Rum and Raisin iz worser than
maggot jam. 4 Seegulls ONLY)

SCOWLING MARGARET'S ADDRESS BOOK OF SEA WIZARDS

Moany Angela

Cave of Black Despair

Shetland

Roaring Jago

Crotchety Cove

Penzance

Whimpering Dave

Sorrow Grotto

Norfolk

Furious Karen

Sludge-hole

London Bridge

The Thames

Moody Maude

Cavern of Whinge

Aberystwyth

SILLY SEA JOKES

How do you cut the sea in two?
With a sea-saw!

Why wouldn't the clam share?
Because he was shell-fish.

What is the strongest creature in the ocean?
A mussel.

What sort of hair do mermaids have?
Wavy.

Why did the crab blush?
Because the sea weed.

Dear Picklewitch,

I am riteing to tell you that I will be out
of badger jail very soon.

I've learned lots of things inside;
like how to knit my own fur, healthy
cooking with wurms and being a
Responsible Garden Citizen.

Please tell the squirrels that I
haven't forgotten who snitched to the
badger police.

See you all soon,
Love from Basher Crunch xx

CLAIRE BARKER
Picklewitch and Jack
A story about two very unlikely friends!
Illustrated by Teemu Juhani

Have you read Picklewitch and Jack's first adventure?

*The dreadful strangers moved in on a
wild and windy Thursday.*

*'Fudgenuts,' cursed Picklewitch, adjusting her
cracked binoculars to get a better view of the
comings-and-goings. 'This won't do at all. I bet they
haven't even bought me any cake.'*

Picklewitch lives in a tree at the bottom of the
garden. She has a nose for naughtiness, a mind
for mischief and a weakness for cake. And
unluckily for brainbox Jack – winner of the
'Most Sensible Boy in School' for the third
year running – she's about to choose him as
her new best friend . . .

CLAIRE BARKER

Picklewitch & Jack
AND THE
CUCKOO COUSIN

He's not all he seems . . .

Illustrated by
Teemu Juhani

Want more excitement?
Meet Picklewitch's cousin . . .

NOBODY tells ME what to do BECUZ . . .
I DUZ what I LIKES and I LIKES what I DUZ
OH YES!

Jack's new best friend Picklewitch is still causing
marvellous mischief. When she receives a letter
from her cousin Archie Cuckoo, telling her
he's coming to stay, Jack worries that she'll lose
interest in him. But this new cousin turns out to
be unexpectedly nice . . .

Unfortunately Archie is not all he seems, and
soon both Picklewitch and Jack realise there
are sinister plans afoot!

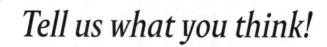

Tell us what you think!

If you enjoyed reading this Faber children's book, help us spread the word!

Tell your family and friends, your local bookshop and leave a review online at one or more of these websites:

▶ **Amazon**   ▶ **Waterstones**

▶ **Goodreads**   ▶ **Toppsta**

Tell us too and join the conversation online
@faberchildrens

Find more books and resources at:
faberchildrens.co.uk

faber